His
Prairie Princess

PRAIRIE BRIDES   BOOK 1

BESTSELLING AUTHOR
KIT MORGAN

ANGEL CREEK PRESS

His Prairie Princess (Prairie Brides, Book One)
© 2013, 2014 Kit Morgan

Cover Design and Interior format by The Killion Group
http://thekilliongroupinc.com

OTHER TITLES BY KIT MORGAN

The Holiday Mail-Order Bride Series
The Christmas Mail-Order Bride
(Holiday Mail-Order Brides, Book One)

The New Year's Bride
(Holiday Mail-Order Brides, Book Two)

His Forever Valentine
(Holiday Mail-Order Brides, Book Three)

Her Irish Surrender (Holiday Mail-Order
Brides, Book Four)

The Springtime Mail-Order Bride
(Holiday Mail-Order Brides, Book Five)

Love in Independence (Holiday Mail-Order
Brides, Book Six)

Love at Harvest Moon
(Holiday Mail-Order Brides, Book Seven)

The Thanksgiving Mail-Order Bride
(Holiday Mail-Order Brides, Book Eight)

The Holiday Mail-Order Bride
(Holiday Mail-Order Brides, Book Nine)

His Mail-Order Valentine
(Holiday Mail-Order Brides, Book Ten)

The Easter Mail-Order Bride
(Holiday Mail-Order Brides, Book Eleven)

A Mid-Summer's Mail-Order Bride
(Holiday Mail Order Brides, Book Twelve)

The Prairie Groom Series
August (Prairie Grooms, Book One)

Ryder (Prairie Grooms, Book Two)

Seth (Prairie Grooms, Book Three)

Chase (Prairie Grooms, Book Four)

Levi (Prairie Grooms, Book Five)

Bran (Prairie Grooms, Book Six)

**The Dalton Brides with
Kirsten Osbourne and Cassie Hayes**
The Escape (A Prologue) by Kit Morgan,
Kirsten Osbourne, Cassie Hayes

The Rancher's Mail-Order Bride by Kirsten Osbourne

The Cowboy's Mail-Order Bride by Kit Morgan

The Drifter's Mail-Order Bride by Cassie Hayes

Hank's Rescued Bride by Cassie Hayes

Benedict's Bargain Bride by Kirsten Osbourne

Percy's Unexpected Bride by Kit Morgan

"There's just something about a western. They're so simple. Good versus evil. The cowboy or lawman has to save the girl then gets the girl. You don't need to dress them up; their purity alone tells a simple story that always satisfies. That's why I love westerns."

~John Terleski

ONE

Oregon Territory, March 1858

"Let's just kill her and be done with it!"

Sadie Jones cringed. Kill her? What did they mean, kill her? The idiots just tied her up – why bother if they were going to kill her anyway?

"Ah, now why wouldja wanna kill a purty thing like this fer? I know a *much* better use fer her! After all, it's why we took her in the first place, ain't it?"

Two of her captors laughed and leered in her direction. Oh, no! Not *that!*

"I still say killin' her is our best option."

"But Jeb!" complained another. "Think of the horrible waste! Ya gotta admit, she's mighty pretty!"

Now all four of them leered, including Jeb.

Her eyes widened. *No, no, please!* She didn't want to end her life like this – raped and murdered by a gang of dirty, stinking, halfwit outlaws!

Thankfully, one of the men's stomachs growled, loudly. They looked at each other, then at their bellies. If Sadie's guess was right, her life was about to be spared by a pot of beans.

"Well, I dunno about y'all, but I can't think on an empty stomach," one moaned, confirming her assumption. She slumped in her chair in relief. "And I'm plumb tired of wearin' this here mask!" he added, adjusting the bandana that still covered the lower half of his face. They'd been wearing them ever since they robbed the stage several hours ago.

"Cain's right. I'm starved, and she can't see us if'n we're in the other room eatin'. Let's go."

Jeb, the leader of the gang, studied her a moment longer before giving in. "All right, let's get some grub. She ain't going anywhere. And later, it won't matter if she sees us. As soon as we're all done with her, she'll be half-dead anyway – we can draw straws to see who gets to finish the job."

They laughed, slapped each other on the back in a congratulatory manner and, spurs jangling, headed into the main room of their cabin hideout.

Sadie Jones took a deep breath through her nose, and grimaced. The odor from the gag they'd placed on her was atrocious! She continued to make a face at the awful smell and let her breath out slowly.

Trussed up, gagged, and stuck with four lecherous outlaws. Lovely. How was she going to get out of this? She should have listened to her father and never set foot outside her door! Why had she gone off by herself? *Why?*

Because she was a headstrong, stubborn, fiercely independent girl, that's why – traits her father said would get her into a lot of trouble. And now they had. Whatever was she to do?

When the outlaws had robbed the stage, she'd figured that was that – her money would be gone and her quest cut short. Worse, she'd have to contact her father and face his wrath over her brash behavior. She was supposed to be heading to her aunt and uncle's ranch for a visit, not gallivanting across the prairie in the opposite direction, in search of her mother.

Guilt suddenly assailed her. Her father didn't suspect a thing. Days, even weeks could pass before he got word from her aunt that she hadn't made it. Sadie had set off on the four-day journey just as she had on past visits, but when the stage caught up with a wagon train, the temptation was too much. She left the stagecoach and paid one of the families in the wagon train to take her along, at least until they came to a point where she could catch a stage to the little town of Clear Creek in the Oregon Territory. It worked, too, until said stage had been held up. But Sadie had never expected to be taken along with the rest of the loot. Being abducted was the last thing on her mind that morning.

Unfortunately it was the foremost thing on it that afternoon.

Sadie again tried the ropes used to lash her hands behind her back and tie her to a chair. No use. They were too tight. She was a helpless captive. So helpless, in fact, that she did something she hadn't done in a very long time. She began to cry.

It wasn't so much out of fear, though she was sure she'd succumb to it when the men came back. No, these tears were out of anger: anger at herself for not heeding her father's advice to wait for him to wrap up a business deal before he could help find her mother. Her *real* mother. But she knew that once her father got around to finishing things up and making their travel arrangements, her mother would be out of time, and out of luck. Death usually didn't give second chances. And, according to a letter her father had received, death was obviously closing in on her. Not the same way it was closing in on Sadie now, but once you're dead, what did it matter?

Sadie closed her eyes. It was her fault for taking off in the first place. She wanted to meet her mother before she died, but it looked like that wasn't going to happen. Her mother would be taken to glory by whatever sort of disease was slowly eating away at her. And Sadie would meet a similar fate, at the hands of four men who thankfully had more interest in a pot of beans at the moment than in her. But those beans weren't going to last the scoundrels much longer …

So Sadie, being a practical girl, did the only thing she could think of considering her current predicament. She sniffed back her tears, bowed her head and prayed that she'd be ready for whatever happened when the beans ran out.

~ ~ ~

Harrison Cooke crawled out of his hiding spot underneath the cabin's porch and crouched beneath a window. He'd followed the outlaws' trail for hours before finally catching up with them. The driver of the stage was badly injured, and it galled Harrison to have to fetch a nearby farmer to tend him. But he couldn't leave the man – then he'd be no better than the thieving scoundrels who'd beat him half to death.

He pushed the thought aside as he slowly stood to peek in the window. The outlaws were all inside as far as he could tell, their horses unsaddled and put in a makeshift corral. He figured they'd been here at least an hour and had possibly settled in for the night. He could smell beans cooking and hear laughter. The scum were probably slugging down shots of whiskey and counting the minutes until they opened the strongbox and mailbag they'd stolen. That is, if they hadn't already.

But he hadn't heard any shots fired or sounds of forcing the lock – and he'd been under the porch for at least half an hour. The strongbox must still be intact. He hoped the mail fared as well, since that was what he was after – specifically, letters from Washington regarding his brothers' pardons. Harrison was prepared to do whatever he had to in order to get them. His two brothers were not going to spend another minute in that rancid, disgusting prison if he could help it!

He took a deep breath and carefully looked again through the dirty window. "What the bloody...," he whispered in shock. "No, it couldn't be."

He turned from the window, shut his eyes tight, then opened them and peeked through the glass again. They had a *woman* tied up in there! Now what was he going to do? His only goal was to retrieve the mailbag; he wasn't equipped to deal with a hostage!

Granted, the stagecoach driver had mentioned a passenger. But Harrison and the farmer had figured that if there was one (unlikely, for who on Earth *wanted* to come to Clear Creek?), the fool must have wandered off after the stage was robbed. That being the case, the passenger could fend for himself; the driver had a more pressing problem. Besides, come suppertime the missing passenger would likely find his way to the farmer's house, as it was the only one in the area. It was amazing how an empty stomach could help a man's sense of direction.

The passenger's real problem, as Harrison saw it now, was that *he* was actually a *she* – and she had been taken from the stage along with the strongbox and mail. With women being exceedingly scarce in these parts, and these outlaws not exactly being church deacons, it didn't bode well for her. He closed his eyes and said a quick prayer that he would get to her before the outlaws did, not to mention get them both out alive and unharmed.

He looked at the closed door leading to the cabin's main room. Voices and raucous laughter could be heard coming from the other side. The mailbag was more than likely there. Then he looked at the woman. Even in the dim light from a nearby lantern he saw she was young, and frightened. Her eyes, a dark blue, were wide over the gag and filled with tears. She wore a simple white bonnet, from which her hair had escaped in tiny dark tendrils about her face. The rest of her ensemble was a white blouse and dark wool skirt – any coat, shawl, or other covering must still be on the stage with her belongings. She had to be half-frozen from the ride to the ramshackle cabin.

Her boots were practical and dirty – they looked like she'd done a lot of walking in them. He briefly wondered if she'd come from one of the wagon trains that passed through to the south. They were also tightly lashed together at her ankles. *Crumbs!* He certainly hoped she had some feeling left in her tiny feet and ankles. She was going to need them in a moment, to run for her life.

Harrison pulled a Bowie knife from the scabbard on his belt. It was the only weapon he had on him. He'd been in such a hurry to meet the stage, he hadn't bothered to change out of his dirty work clothes or put on his gun belt. Despite being an excellent shot he didn't wear a gun often; pig farming didn't much call for it. But he'd gladly carry one from now on if he managed to get out of this.

He took one last look at the woman. Her head was bowed and her body shook, either with silent sobs or from the cold. Either way, it didn't matter – the sight still made his gut twist. He gritted his teeth and quietly backed away.

Now he needed a diversion, something to draw the outlaws away from the cabin long enough to rescue the woman and retrieve the mailbag. He looked at his surroundings. It was already dark, and getting colder by the minute. The bit of snow on the ground, coupled with the scant light from the crescent moon, would help, but it was still going to be difficult to get himself and the woman to his horse without a lantern to light the way.

Harrison took in his surroundings for another brief moment before he suddenly smiled. Of course, why hadn't he thought of it before? He had just the thing to use for a distraction …

Sadie's head hung low, her chin on her chest. She watched her tears fall into her lap and tried to keep from shivering. It had been easy to stop crying when she was angry with herself. But the sound of chairs being pushed away from a table, deep male laughter and plenty of belching told her that she was about to be served up on a silver platter – or in this case, probably the dirty wooden floor her chair sat on.

The only furniture in the room she occupied was the chair she was tied to and a small wooden barrel with a lantern on it. Was there was a third room with an actual bed inside? It might be nicer to die on a bed and not the floor, or the kitchen table. Perhaps the third room was through the door directly behind her. She'd noticed it when they shoved her into the chair and tied her up.

Oh, what was she thinking? *Stop it, Sadie, stop it!* She was the daughter of a cattle baron, for Heaven's sake! She'd come north from Texas with her father when she was five, when the war with Mexico started, and had helped him settle in the Oregon territory after her stepmother had died. He'd become one of the major names in the beef industry, had brought commerce to the wilds of Oregon, supplied the wagon trains and helped tame the prairies.

And the whole time, she'd been right by his side, working almost as hard as he had. She could shoot a gun. She could brand a steer. She'd been on a cattle drive. And, by God, she wasn't going to go down without a fight and have her father think of her as some weak, stupid female who couldn't take care of business!

Of course, if she survived this, she'd still have to hear about not listening to him. And taking off by herself across the prairie. And getting abducted, of course. But it would be a small price to pay …

Her head snapped up. A sound suddenly caught her attention. A horrible howl carried on the wind sent a chill up her spine. *Wolves?* Her eyes darted to the door. Her captors heard it too, if the dead quiet in the other room was an indication.

Another sound caught Sadie's attention, this one much different. A horse was running past her window – she could hear the hoofbeats loud and clear.

Another wolf howl rent the air, closer this time.

"The horses! Those stinkin' varmints are goin' after the horses!" one of the men cried. There was a mad scramble on the other side of the door. She heard their cursing along with the sound of booted feet stomping every which way but out the front door. They weren't the most organized lot, and she thanked the Lord for that. It might buy her some time.

Finally, after several more sets of racing hoof beats, further stomping and cursing, and the sound of a door being thrown open, the cabin went silent.

"Don't move a muscle and don't make a sound," a deep, accented voice hissed in her ear from behind. Where did he come from? She hadn't even heard him enter the room! She saw a flash of steel out the corner of one eye. A knife – a really *big* knife! *No! Oh, no, please!* One of them had stayed behind, and was going to take her before the others had a chance.

"I hope you've enough strength in you for what's to come," he whispered as he began to saw through the ropes used to tie her to the chair. "But don't worry, we'll be quick about it. They won't know until it's too late."

Sadie's tears fell in force, blurring her vision. Where had her bravery gone? And oh! – the man stunk to high Heaven. He smelled   of   mud,   straw, and … was that pig?

He grabbed her from behind and yanked her out of the chair.

Nooooo! Sadie's entire body shook with terror. She couldn't breathe, couldn't see and, for the first time in her life, couldn't stay conscious …

TWO

The woman landed on the floor like a sack of potatoes. Harrison had barely let go of her to untie her ankles when she toppled over in a dead faint. He glanced quickly around. Blast it, the outlaws could be back any minute!

There was only one thing to do. He picked her up, threw her over his shoulder and – since he couldn't very well use the bedroom window he'd crawled through to get into the cabin – headed for the back door. But to get to it, he realized, he'd have to go through the main room …

He carefully opened the door and looked for any sign of the mailbag. Nothing! Where could it be?

A horse ran past the open front door. A shout soon followed.

Harrison had no choice. He had to escape! Tightening his hold on the woman, he made for the rear door on the other side of the room, checked for any signs of the outlaws, and then ran into the cold night.

He almost slipped on an icy patch of snow, but managed to keep his feet under him. The woman was blissfully light, thank the Lord for that! But even so, he would have to carry her a good distance, and over time he would eventually tire. Especially if it took him a while to find his own horse in the dark …

He had begun to wonder if the woman had regained consciousness when he heard another shout in the distance. He pushed himself harder, stumbled again and ran sidelong into a tree, shoulder first. He grimaced as he hit, and hoped the audible *thud* he'd heard wasn't the woman's head. But then, what else could it be? If she had woken up, that blow would have put her right out again. The only consolation was that it was certainly a better fate for her than what the outlaws had planned. Regardless, once they were safe he could take her straight to Doc Waller in Clear Creek.

Harrison kept moving until he heard the sound of water and headed for it. He'd hobbled his horse near a small stream, and the animal couldn't be far off. He carried the still form down to the bank, stopped to catch his breath, then risked a low whistle. His mare Juliet nickered in return. It was faint, but it was enough, and he took off downstream toward the sound. After a few moments he found Juliet right where he'd left her.

Just in time, too. It was starting to snow.

"OK, darling – you're going to have to take it from here," he whispered to Juliet as he hefted his load across the saddle. It was a horrible way to transport the woman, but he wasn't sure he had time to untie her and bring her around. Who knew how close those outlaws might be? He quickly mounted, lifted her body to slide into the saddle himself and laid her across his lap as best he could. It was going to be a rough ride with her body wedged between his torso and the saddle horn, but at least she would stay put.

With one hand on the woman and the other holding the reins, he kicked Juliet into action and they were off across the stream, through the woods and, none too soon, heading for the open prairie. This was the one place he feared they might be caught. A couple inches of snow covered the ground, and even though the crescent moon gave little light, it would probably be enough for the outlaws to track them. He needed to get some distance from them. With luck, it would snow enough soon to hide any trail he'd left.

Harrison slowed Juliet and turned to check the landscape behind them. Nothing. No light in the trees, no dark forms coming across the snow. By now the outlaws must've caught their horses and discovered that the woman was gone. Even if they had been dumb enough not to guard her, they weren't so dumb they wouldn't notice her bonds had been cut, the "wolf pack" nothing but a diversion.

But after a few more minutes, he took another quick look at the dark line of pine bordering the prairie. It was snowing harder now, but not so hard he couldn't see the light of a lantern flashing through the trees.

They were coming.

He had a good head start, but was it enough? They might still see him. Taking the woman straight to Doc Waller, then, was out of the question – Juliet would never make the extra miles to town if he pushed her much harder. He wished he'd taken his brother's stallion, Romeo – a race across the open prairie would be no problem then – but he'd only planned to get the mail, not rescue a damsel in distress! He could still lose them in the gentle rolling landscape of the prairie – the outlaws wouldn't be able to keep a steady eye on him. Unfortunately, he wouldn't be able to keep an eye on them either.

He stopped briefly to take in his surroundings. The farm was closer. Juliet could make it with no problem, and at least his stepbrothers and father would be there. They could help protect the woman … maybe. It would depend on how much they'd been drinking. In fact, the more he thought about it, he might have to protect her from his stepbrothers and father as well. None of them had been around a woman in a long time; the only "soiled dove" in the area was indisposed, and not a very good one at that. The others had been run out of town.

That left only one choice.

Harrison groaned at the thought and took off again, this time toward home. He prayed as Juliet naturally picked up her pace: *Father, please forgive me for what I must do. And please, Lord, may this woman forgive me, too.*

Sadie tried to open her eyes. The effort was painful. In fact, every part of her body hurt – her limbs ached, her head felt like it was about to explode, her stomach was cramping. Where was she? The last thing she could remember was …

She didn't seem to have any memory at all! Maybe it was because the effort it took to think hurt too much.

She decided to try and figure out where she currently was instead of where she'd been. But when she attempted to move, she found she was held in place. She was on her back, that was certain, and it was dark, and she could smell hay. In fact, she was not only lying on a bed of hay, she was covered with blankets of it.

Sadie tried to roll over, move, anything, but couldn't. Finally she realized she was still bound and gagged.

Oh, Lord, no! Memories came trickling back: the stagecoach, the outlaws, the ... *rescue*? Is that what happened? Where was the man who freed her from the chair? She must have fainted, but how long does a faint last? And where was she now?

She vaguely remembered being carried through the dark. She remembered the cold. In fact, she was still cold, but not like before. But if she'd been rescued, why was she still tied up? And why did her head feel like it was about to shatter like glass?

A door creaked and groaned. Sadie froze. *If I'm about to die, Lord, let it be quick. I feel terrible enough as it is.*

Booted footsteps. A man. There was a rustle of hay and before she could even scream into the gag, he was almost upon her!

But he didn't grab her as she expected. Instead, he was very gentle, removing the hay that was covering her. Then he stood and lit a lantern.

His back to her as he hung the lamp on a peg, she quickly studied him. He was as tall and broad as some of her father's cowhands; she could tell by his frame that he'd known hard work. His hair was a sable brown, much like hers, and just reached the collar of his coat. When he turned, his dark eyes widened as he looked at her. No, not at her – *into* her, right into her very soul. It made her feel incredibly vulnerable. Being helplessly bound certainly didn't help, either.

"Oh, good – you're awake," he whispered. "I wasn't sure if you would be. Your head … I'm so sorry, but it took quite a blow."

Her eyes widened. He had an accent … English, maybe, or perhaps New England. Who was this man? She struggled briefly in her bonds, but the pain stopped her.

"Oh, dear! I'm so sorry – let me help you." He reached behind him and pulled out a huge knife. Sadie automatically shook her head.

"No, I won't hurt you, I promise. I'm here to help. I do apologize for not untying you earlier – I was in a bit of a hurry …" He gently pulled her up to a sitting position.

Her head swam, and she fell against his shoulder as he reached behind her and began to cut the rope binding her wrists. She belatedly realized she was wrapped in several blankets – of cloth, not just straw. No wonder she wasn't as cold as before.

"I'll free you, but you must promise me to stay calm. I cannot help you if you start to scream and panic. Do you understand?"

He was warm, and didn't smell as bad as before. He had to be the same man who took her from the outlaw's cabin. He spoke with the same odd accent and still had the scent of livestock on him, particularly pig. She knew that smell – they had kept pigs at home.

The ranch. Her father ... Sadie moaned.

"There, there. You'll be all right." He tossed the rope aside and took a moment to study her in the soft lantern light. His eyes widened and his breath caught. He collected himself, and quickly began to untie her ankles.

Sadie let herself fall against him as he worked, too tired to care about the contact. He was wonderfully warm. The sensation brought comfort and eased the pain that throbbed throughout her entire body.

He returned her to a sitting position. "You promise you won't scream?"

She nodded. It hurt.

He reached behind her head and untied the bandana. She nearly choked when he removed it, her stomach suddenly sick.

She must have looked ill, for he quickly took her in his arms and cradled her against him, beginning to rock gently. "You're going to be all right," he said as he looked down into her eyes. "I'll take you to town to see the doctor. Then we can find the sheriff – he should be back by now. He's been hunting an outlaw gang, possibly the same ones who abducted you. Would you like some water?"

She stared back. His face was bent over hers, his eyes conveying a warmth no number of blankets could produce. It was a look she had never seen before and couldn't quite put a name to. She licked her dry lips. "Water …"

Without taking his eyes off her, he reached behind himself and grabbed a small canteen. He opened it and held it to her lips. "There, there, not too much. Take small sips."

She took little gulps instead. It was a mistake – she immediately turned and retched into the hay.

"Not to worry, not to worry! Let me help you." He pulled a handkerchief out of his back pocket, poured some water onto it, and cleaned her face as if it was the most natural thing he could do. "I dare say, but you're in a bad way. I've got to get you to Dr. Waller."

Sadie looked at him. "Who are you?" she croaked.

"Oh! I'm terribly sorry – Harrison Cooke, at your service. And you are?"

A raspy whisper. "Sadie Jones."

"Would you like to try some more water, Miss Jones? Perhaps just to rinse your mouth this time? Or a little sip?"

She did one, then the other. It was better. The water stayed down.

"You've been through a horrible ordeal, Miss Jones. I'm terribly sorry you've suffered so."

She looked him over with what strength she had left. "What are you doing here?"

"I've come to help you, of course."

"No. I mean, what are you doing here in Oregon Territory? Where are you from?"

"Oh ... yes, well. I hail from Sussex originally. My family came here in 1846, when this was still British territory – or at least disputed," he added with a wry smile.

"An Englishman?" Sadie whispered, and put a hand to her head in an attempt to still the throbbing.

"Here now, lie back. There's a good girl. I'm going to get the wagon ready and take you to Dr. Waller."

"What happened to me?" she asked as the room began to spin.

"You were abducted by outlaws. I rescued you and brought you here."

"To a ... *barn*?"

"Er, yes. A barn. Trust me, it's much better than the alternative. We'd best see to your head now." He gently covered her with the blankets again, then poured more water on the handkerchief, folded it, and placed it on her forehead.

The cool cloth felt good. Sadie closed her eyes, her body heavy with exhaustion. Sleep began to pull at her. And his voice was like soft silk against her raw nerves. "Now, dear princess, let's see about getting you to the doctor ..."

THREE

Harrison wanted to kick himself for such a forward statement. "Princess? Really?" he mumbled as he tucked the blankets around her. She had fallen asleep quickly – perhaps too quickly, considering her ordeal. He knew a little about this sort of thing, enough to know that it was dangerous for someone to drift in and out. He'd watched it happen to his own father. But when his father had fallen asleep after hitting his head in a carriage accident, he'd never woken up again.

In short, he had to hurry.

But despite his need to get the woman to town, he couldn't help but take a few seconds to study Miss Sadie Jones. Her dark lashes were long and beautiful against her pale skin, her lips a delicate pink. A lock of hair had fallen across her face, and he gently brushed it away, reveling in the softness of her cheek. She was beautiful. Perhaps calling her "princess" was appropriate – she certainly looked like one. A sleeping beauty he could awaken with a kiss …

Get a hold of yourself, man! He tore his gaze away. His stomach knotted with a pang of unfamiliar emotion, one much different from when he'd seen her tied to a chair. That was righteous anger over the outlaws' cruel treatment of her. This was desire, a deep, possessive desire that rose up with incomprehensible force as he knelt beside her. It scared him.

The outlaws had intended to harm her in the worst possible way. If he hadn't gone to meet the stage, then set out after the mailbag, she'd likely be dead. That scared him even more.

He chuckled to himself as he stood. His sleeping princess hadn't been saved by a kiss, but by a piece of mail intended to save his brothers – a piece of mail he still needed to find. But he had to take care of Miss Jones first. She was still in danger from her injury, not to mention the outlaws until they were safely behind bars. He vowed to make sure the scum wouldn't get anywhere near her in the meantime, even if it meant putting them behind bars himself.

But it wasn't only the outlaws he needed to protect her from. He had to hurry and get her to town before his stepbrothers and stepfather discovered her in the barn. They were just as bad, maybe even worse – as he'd suspected, they'd been drinking.

Harrison walked to an old trunk where his gun belt lay, picked it up and put it on, then went to hitch up the wagon to take his sleeping princess to safety.

Sadie awoke to the jangle of harness, and hoofbeats crunching on the snow. It was cold, bitterly so, at least on her face. The rest of her was wrapped snugly in a pile of quilts and blankets from the barn.

She had to blink her eyes a few times against the morning light before she could see. The sun was coming up to her left, the sky a dark blue. They had to be heading north, presumably to Clear Creek and the doctor.

She again lay on a bed of hay, and was glad for it – its softness helped to cushion her aching body from the ruts in the road. She took some time to figure out what to do once they got to town. She'd have to talk to the sheriff, of course, and let the doctor tend her – those things came first. But then she needed to inquire about her mother. She must still be alive, she had to be!

And after she found her, she could send word to her father. That wasn't going to be pleasant no matter how she looked at it. At least she would have time with her mother before the famous Horatio Jones came riding into town like a tornado to whisk her back to his cattle kingdom. But she would insist they take her mother with them. She couldn't bear it if her mother was still deathly ill and her father turned his back on her. He'd done that once already.

Sadie knew the story – a few months ago, Maria, the family cook, had told her everything. Maria had been with the Jones family since Sadie's father was a boy and remembered his trip to Paso del Norte before his engagement, to sow his wild oats before he got hogtied into matrimony. A few years later, however, it became evident that his new wife was barren.

It was also quite evident that Horatio Jones had a daughter – or so said a letter he'd received, saying to come get the babe if he had any interest in her. The note had come from an El Paso madam named Bess, who was planning to head to the Oregon Territory.

Horatio, as it turned out, had bedded down with a Mexican merchant's daughter. The act had ruined her, and cast out by her family, she'd had only one option to stay alive. She quickly became a fine addition to Bess's establishment, a radiant beauty and very popular with the gents, but it wasn't long before they found out she was pregnant.

Had she not been such a beauty, Bess might've thrown her out on the streets. But the madam was already planning her trip north, and knew she'd be worth her weight in gold along the trail and into Oregon, where women – especially exotic-looking women like herself – were few and far between. Men would pay good money to have her, and lots of it. A child would only complicate things.

Thankfully, Bess had a soft spot for the tyke, and knew who the father was. But out on the frontier, you had to be practical.

The upshot was that Bess would let her "girl" keep the baby until it came time to leave, but she wouldn't be allowed to take it along. If she wanted to hang onto her job, she'd have to get rid of it.

Of course, Horatio Jones had no idea that Sadie knew. Both he and her stepmother, Ellie, had told her she was orphaned by her birth mother when she joined a wagon train to Oregon, that Horatio had rescued her and brought her home to be raised by the childless couple. That was true – or more correctly, half-true. They left out the part about her mother being a whore, and her father being her actual father.

"We're almost there. Are you feeling any better?"

Sadie turned her head slightly. Her own rescuer was out of her line of vision, but she heard him well enough. "A little. Can we go to the sheriff first?"

"Good Lord, no! You're in no shape to see the sheriff just yet. I'm taking you straight to Dr. Waller. Everything else can wait."

His manners surprised her, and his accent was charming. He was a delightful contrast to the rough and dirty cowhands around her father's ranch; half of them didn't even speak English, and the other half only did so punctuated with crudities. Harrison Cooke looked the part of a rough cowhand or farmer, but he certainly didn't act or speak like one.

He stopped the wagon in front of a small, two-story, whitewashed house at the edge of town. She looked over the town of Clear Creek as he carefully helped her out of the wagon and carried her toward the house. There was only one street, with three or four buildings on either side, a livery stable at the far end, and a few small houses at the near one. There wasn't even a church or schoolhouse that she could see.

It was a far cry from El Paso, she thought. Granted, El Paso only had a few hundred people, but there was still the river traffic and merchants coming over from the much larger town of Paso del Norte on the Mexican side of the border. On the ranch, "going to town" meant at least a little taste of civilization. She'd assumed she'd given that up in coming to Oregon, but she had expected more than … this!

Her rescuer carried her to the door and tapped on it with his boot. She heard footsteps approach from the other side, and the door opened. "Harrison Cooke! What have you got there?" a tall, thin older woman asked. "Quick now, bring her in before the wind gets into my bones."

He brought Sadie into the house. Warmth immediately wrapped around her, bringing with it the delicious smells of fresh-baked bread, bacon and coffee. Her stomach rumbled louder than the outlaws' had the night before, much to her embarrassment.

"Heavens, what a sound! When was the last time you ate, child?"

Harrison gently set Sadie on her feet but didn't let go. "If my guess is right, not since yesterday morning," he answered for her. "She was on the stage when it was robbed."

The woman gasped and took her from his arms. "Are you hurt? What happened?"

"I think I'm all right now. But I am terribly hungry, and cold."

"Let's get you some food, then. I just took some bread out of the oven, and the kitchen's nice and warm." She began to steer Sadie toward the wonderful smell of food. "You'll find Doc out back, Harrison. Best go fetch him."

He tipped his hat and hurried out the door.

The woman led Sadie down a short hall to the kitchen, settled her at the table and got her a cup of coffee. Sadie took it gratefully and held the cup between her hands to let the warmth sink in. It was heaven.

"Your name, child," the woman stated rather than asked as she began to slice some bread.

"Sadie. Sadie Jones."

"Sarah Waller. But everyone around here calls me Grandma."

"Everyone?"

"Oh, yes. I'm the oldest living soul in town, even older than Mr. Waller. Settled here when our wagon broke down, along with a few other families – including Harrison and the rest of that brood of Cookes. Been here a good eight years now."

"What brought an English family out west?"

The woman stopped slicing a moment. "Well, Harrison's father died in St. Louis. He and his wife and sons were coming out west to raise cattle, but he had some sort of accident. The mother remarried to survive,

I suppose, and brought her three sons out here along with her new husband and his two boys. Harrison was probably seventeen at the time."

"Where are you from?"

"Kansas – a little town called Lawrence. Mr. Waller got it in his head to do his doctoring in Oregon City, but this is as far as we got. We both fell in love with the prairie and the nearby mountains. It's not like Kansas prairie, mind you, but we knew we belonged here. Besides, from what I've heard since, Lawrence isn't exactly a hospitable place anymore. Here, have some bread and bacon – you must be half-starved, and here I am flapping my gums!" She set a plate in front of Sadie.

The only thing that kept Sadie from wolfing down the food that moment was Harrison returning with the doctor. They headed straight for her, but Doc Waller, a wiry little man with white hair, stopped up short, his mouth half opened, and stared.

Sadie looked from one man to the other. What could be wrong? Harrison wasn't looking at her so strangely.

Doc Waller glanced at his wife, then back to Sadie, and now both studied her with interest.

"It's her head I'm concerned about, Doctor," Harrison said, interrupting their scrutiny. "She took a frightful hit."

"For Heaven's sake, child," Mrs. Waller began as she handed Harrison a cup of coffee. "Why didn't you say so? A head injury can be dangerous!"

"I don't think it's so bad. I feel much better than last night," Sadie volunteered.

"I'll be the judge of that," Doc Waller said firmly. "Take off that bonnet. It looks like it needs a good washing anyway."

"Yes, sir," said Sadie, setting the half-eaten bread on the plate as he came around the table. When she complied, her hair spilled out of the bonnet in a dark cascade, loose pins tinkling onto the floor.

Harrison had just taken a sip of his coffee, and almost choked.

"Steady there, son," Doc Waller commented knowingly and began to examine her head.

It didn't take long to find the spot. "Oh!" Sadie exclaimed when he touched the large lump.

"Ooh, that's a doozy – maybe the biggest lump I've ever come across. How'd you get it?"

Now Harrison did choke.

"I don't remember."

"Hmmm," Doc began. "You wouldn't happen to know anything about it, would you Harrison?"

Harrison set his coffee down. "Ah, yes. Well, as it was, Miss Jones ... she ... well, I had to ... what I mean to say ..."

"Spit it out, boy!"

Harrison looked at Sadie. "I do so apologize." He turned to Doc Waller, his face reddening. "I accidentally ... ran her into a tree."

"You ... you did *wha-a-a-at*?" Doc Waller sputtered.

Sadie sat and stared at him, eyes wide.

Harrison squared his shoulders. "I had to carry you after you fainted. As I was fleeing, I slipped on some ice, and fell against a tree. I'm afraid, Miss Jones, your head hit it harder than I did. Please, dear lady, accept my most humble apologies."

"That'd do it," Doc Waller mumbled as he began to feel around the injured area again.

Sadie continued to sit and stare. So he really had rescued her – okay, clumsily, but rescued her nonetheless. She knew she was delirious last night, and thought she might have imagined parts of it. But she hadn't. It must have been horrific for him to carry her while running for his life as he escaped to his horse, or wagon, or … oh, the details didn't matter! What did matter was that he had risked his life to save her, and succeeded. A bump on the head was a small price to pay. "Thank you," she told him softly.

Harrison gave her a single, nervous nod and smile. "Well, then … I'd, um, best go see if I can find the sheriff." He quickly darted from the room.

Sadie could only nod at his retreating back as Doc Waller continued to poke and prod her skull. The enormity of her recent ordeal was hitting her full force. She would be forever grateful to the broad-shouldered Englishman who'd saved her life.

Not only that, but he'd also saved her quest. "Dr. Waller? Do you know a woman here in town by the name of Teresa Menendez?"

"I don't know of any Miss Menendez. There is a woman in town named Teresa, but …" He trailed off.

Mrs. Waller's mouth formed into a thin line. "Here now, girl – what business do you have with the likes of her?"

Sadie ignored her tone. "Do you know her?"

The Wallers exchanged a quick glance as Doc came around the table to stand next to his wife. "We both know *of* her," he answered.

"But what would you want with her, dear?" Mrs. Waller importuned. "She's a harlot, child – a harlot! You've no business even going near a woman like that!"

"Sarah, hush now!" Doc Waller ordered.

Mrs. Waller's words stung, but Sadie's resolve was firm. She took a deep breath. "Is she alive?"

"Yep, I reckon so," he began. "That is, the last time I checked. But … why? What's she to you?"

"Perhaps to you, she's nothing more than a harlot. But to me …" Sadie looked them in the eye. "… she's my mother."

FOUR

"Your mother?" Mrs. Waller gasped.

"Blazes, Sarah, of course! I knew she looked familiar – I just didn't know why. Now that you mention it, you can see it plain as day ..."

"Well, yes, I can see it! But did she know her mother was a ... a ..."

Sadie was getting close to having had enough of this. "An adventurous woman, Mrs. Waller?" she finished the sentence. "A prostitute? A courtesan? A whore? Yes. Yes, I know."

Mrs. Waller stood and stammered as she searched for the best way to apologize. Finally she said, "I'm sorry if I offended you. Guess it don't much matter what she's done – she's still your mama. And it's none of my business, anyway – it's just that ... well, decent folk around here ran the rest of those women out of town. They left your mother behind on account of her being ill. Only a matter of time before she'd be run out, too, only no one wanted to be responsible."

"Responsible for what?"

Mrs. Waller closed her eyes a moment. "Her passing on."

Sadie stood. That made sense – driving a sick woman out of town in this cold would be a death sentence. "Can you take me to her?"

"Well ..." Doc Waller was clearly reluctant. "After that knock to the noggin, you really should be resting. But if you feel you're up to it ..."

"I do," Sadie interrupted.

"Then we can go right now if you like."

"Or at least after you finish eating," Mrs. Waller added.

"Thank you. I would appreciate it. And no offense taken – I know what my mother is." Sadie took another bite of bread and tried to collect herself. How could people be so cruel to another human being? The townspeople here had no idea what had made her mother sink to such desperation. *But I know*, she thought to herself. "More than anything else, I want to be able to tell her I love her before she dies. She is dying, isn't she, Doc?"

Doc Waller slowly nodded.

Tears stung the back of Sadie's eyes, but she refused to let them have their way. "Let's go, then. I can eat on the way."

Within minutes, Sadie was on her way to meet a woman she could not remember. She had no idea what she looked like – except vaguely like her, according to the Wallers – or what kind of person she was before her ruin, or if the woman even loved her. But one thing she did know was how much it could mean to someone to let them know they were loved. And even if her mother would not, or could not, tell her how she felt about her, she desperately needed to tell her mother she loved her. And forgave her, if anything needed to be forgiven.

Perhaps then, Sadie could find it in her heart to forgive her father.

Harrison hurried down the street to the sheriff's office, the look on Miss Jones's face still fresh in his mind. It had changed from accusatory to admiring as she realized what he'd done. He was right – a bump to the head was much better in her eyes than being dead at the hands of outlaws.

He smiled as he stepped up to the sheriff's office, and it broadened as he remembered her dark hair, freed from the confines of her bonnet, spilling down around her shoulders. He'd never seen such a beautiful sight. Such a beautiful woman. Such a …

The door was locked, the sheriff's office empty. "Blast!" The posse was probably still out searching for the outlaws.

He focused himself back on the business at hand. He had to find out if the posse had retrieved the mailbag, not to mention those no-good outlaws – but short of riding out alone trying to find them (which would be foolhardy even if it wasn't the middle of winter) he had no way of doing that. Therefore, there was no sense in waiting around. He might as well head back to the Wallers' and see how Miss Jones was faring.

"You're up early, ain't ya?" a voice called.

Harrison turned. His stepbrothers, Jack and Sam, stood on the other side of the street. Great. This was all he needed. He sighed. "I'd say the same for you – you two are never up this early. Is Mulligan giving away free drinks this morning?"

His brothers both sneered at him. "If'n he was, we never woulda come home last night!" Jack called back. Both brothers laughed boisterously at the remark.

Harrison rolled his eyes. It didn't take much to send them into hysterics. "Are you telling me you've actually come into town for a *purpose*?"

Sam settled himself somewhat. "We came for coffee, an' a few other things. Seems *someone* ain't been keeping up on the supplies like he oughta."

"Why else would I be here?" Harrison countered.

"Then how come you're hangin' 'round the sheriff's office? And why's the wagon over by Doc's?" Jack asked, a challenge in his voice.

"Why don't you come across the street and talk to me, instead of doing all this yelling?"

Sam spit. "Worthless piece of ..."

"I've heard the posse will be back soon," Harrison said, changing the subject. "I was wondering if they'd found out anything before I got supplies. You haven't seen them, have you?"

"What do we care?" Sam asked.

"I thought you might be curious, like everyone else. There's been too much thievery of late, don't you think?"

Sam and Jack both spit. "Don't pay it no mind," Sam said. "Get the supplies, then get on home. You got pigs to feed and a barn to clean, boy." He shoved Jack, and they headed down the street toward the livery stable.

Harrison watched them go. Mulligan's was closed, and his lazy brothers never came to town to actually take care of any real business. That was Harrison's job. The only business that brought the other Cooke men to town was drinking. So why were they here at this hour? Hadn't they noticed the wagon was gone? That alone should have indicated he'd come to town to tend to things. And if one of those things had nothing to do with keeping them and their equally unindustrious father provided with caffeine and food ... well, he didn't see that it was any business of theirs. He headed back to the Wallers' and continued to puzzle over his brothers unusual presence.

It wasn't long before he saw Miss Jones walking toward him, the Wallers along with her. He stopped short and watched her approach. He was glad she had an overcoat on – probably the doctor's, as her hands barely peeked out from the long sleeves. She'd not bothered to re-pin her hair, but instead wore it long and loose. By Heaven, she was the most beautiful thing he'd ever seen.

He swallowed hard as she walked up to him. "Mr. Cooke, did you find the sheriff?" she asked.

Harrison's eyes locked on hers. The deep cornflower blue was mesmerizing. "I'm afraid he hasn't returned," he rasped. He hadn't wanted to sound like a blithering idiot, but his mouth had gone dry, and he had to fight the urge to lick his lips. Good God, had it been that long since he'd been around a beautiful woman?

Actually, now that he thought about it, yes, it had. And he wasn't sure he'd ever been around one *this* beautiful before yesterday …

Dr. Waller eyed him and smiled a lopsided grin. Grandma Waller also looked, smiled and quickly glanced at Miss Jones. Egads, was he being *that* obvious? Inwardly, he groaned.

Miss Jones, if she had noticed his starry-eyed expression, was either too polite to comment or too intent on other things. "Just as well. I was going to visit my mother."

Harrison opened his mouth to speak but nothing came out for a moment. There were only so many people in Clear Creek … "Who is your mother?" he finally asked.

"Teresa Menendez. And before you say it, yes, I know." Miss Jones walked on, the Wallers trailing behind.

Harrison turned and watched them go, his mind ticking off a mental list of people he knew in Clear Creek. Which, in this case, was practically everyone. But he didn't recall a Teresa Menendez. Unless … "Do you mean to tell me your mother is Tantaliz–" He snapped his mouth shut, and covered it with his hand. Oh dear …

Miss Jones spun on her heel to face him. Her voice was unraised, but with an edge.

"I'm sorry – what did you call her?"

If he had any sense, Harrison thought, he'd pull his gun out and pistol-whip himself with it – or perhaps shoot his own tongue off. Probably the latter, as it would keep him from making such an error again. "I did not mean to offend, I assure you. But the only person I know of here named Teresa is ..."

"The town whore. Yes, I've been informed," she replied darkly.

Harrison's eyes widened slightly. "Tantalizing

Teresa ... is your mother?"

"Tantalizing. An interesting nickname." If words were knives, she would have just pinned him to the nearest wall.

"It's ... what the men here call her."

"Really? And what have you called her, Mr. Cooke?"

Harrison sighed. She automatically assumed he'd used the services of the only "soiled dove" remaining in Clear Creek. After all, there weren't any other unmarried women in the area. There were blessed few *married* women – Grandma Waller; Irene Dunnigan, who ran the mercantile with her husband, Wilfred; a few farmers' wives; and Mrs. Van Cleet, who had come to Clear Creek with her husband, Cyrus. They planned on building a hotel in the spring, when everything thawed out. The stage came through once a month, but word was it would come more frequently in the very near future. Especially with a hotel in town …

"Well, Mr. Cooke?"

Sadie's voice brought Harrison out of the reverie to which he'd attempted to escape. If he wanted to live, he decided, he had better choose his next words carefully … "To be perfectly frank, I've never made her acquaintance."

Miss Jones sighed in relief. "Well … I suppose that's for the best, don't you think?" She quickly turned and started off again. The Wallers followed.

Harrison walked quickly to catch up as a disturbing thought crossed his mind. There were at least ten men for every woman in the area, and almost all of those women were married. Tantal … er, *Miss Menendez*, was the only "working girl" that hadn't been chased off, and there were no virgin daughters around that he knew of. He had a sudden urge to take the beautiful Miss Jones and whisk her away to safety, to protect her from the potential riot once the men of the region found out an eligible female had arrived!

It wasn't long before they reached the saloon. "According to Mr. Mulligan, Mrs. Dunnigan insisted that, um, Teresa move to the shed out back," Doc Waller informed Sadie. "More privacy. Follow me."

They went around the side of the building to the rear yard. Harrison had never been behind the saloon and was surprised to find a small fenced area that looked like it was used as a vegetable garden. Beyond that area was a tiny shed, no more than seven feet to a side. It had a door and a small window. Many of the shed's boards had knotholes which the wind probably blew right through. Dear heavens, the poor woman had to be freezing in there!

Miss Jones must have thought the same thing. She raced to the shed's door, her face stricken, and softly knocked before entering.

Harrison and the Wallers quickly followed her in. Just as Harrison had guessed, the temperature inside wasn't any different from outside. There was a small pot-bellied stove, but it was stone cold. "I'll start a fire right away," he offered.

"No need, Harrison," Dr. Waller told him, and bent over the cot against the wall.

A thin form was buried beneath several ragged quilts. He gently shook the woman who, in reply, fell into a horrible coughing fit. She poked her head out from under the quilts and spit blood into a nearby bucket, then took in the faces staring down at her. "What do you want?" she rasped.

Miss Jones approached slowly, and the others moved out of her way. She pushed the bucket behind her and knelt beside the cot. "I … I've come to help you."

The woman's glazed eyes narrowed. "Help me?" She coughed again. "Help me out of town, you mean. What's the matter? This shed still too close to Mrs. Dunnigan? I suppose now she wants to send me out onto the prairie to die."

Miss Jones shook her head. "No, no – nothing like that. We're here to take you to Dr. and Mrs. Waller's home. You can get better there. They have a room you can use."

The Wallers exchanged glances. This wasn't part of the plan! And yet …

The woman looked at her and began coughing again, finally spitting more blood into the bucket Miss Jones had been quick to grab. Exhausted, she fell back on the cot. "Who are you?"

Harrison watched as Miss Jones took a deep breath, and said, "I'm your daughter Sadie, and I've come to get you out of here."

FIVE

Sadie held her breath.

Her mother stared at her in shock and disbelief before she clawed her way to a sitting position. Once she managed that, she again began coughing uncontrollably. Doc Waller stepped forward. "We'd best move her before the cold takes its toll. It's freezing in here." He turned to his wife. "You run on ahead and get the bed ready."

Grandma Waller shook off her shock and hurried out the door as the coughing continued.

Sadie extended a hand and began rubbing her mother's back. The woman looked like she was trying to wave her away as her body jerked and heaved from the force of her coughs, but Sadie wouldn't stop. Even if she wasn't her mother, no one should suffer so. "Let's get you out of here. You'll be much more comfortable at the Wallers'."

"Why … are you … doing this?" her mother rasped between spasms.

"I told you. I'm your daughter. You won't get well in this drafty shack. What are you doing out here, anyway?"

The woman hugged herself to get her heaving body under control. "Don't you know? I ain't fit enough to be inside. I'm no better than a filthy animal in this town's eyes."

Sadie motioned to Doc Waller to help get her mother off the cot. She'd deal with the remark about the town later; getting her mother warm was more important.

"Please, let me help," Harrison said. He bent to the cot and, in one swift move, lifted her mother into his arms, quilts and all.

"Mr. Cooke!" Sadie said. Surely he wasn't going to carry her all the way back to the Wallers' home? But then … he'd carried her, for a greater distance and under much more difficult circumstances. She felt an odd flutter in her stomach at the thought of his race to save her from the outlaws.

He looked at her, an eyebrow raised in question, and smiled. "Don't worry. I'll make very sure to avoid trees, I promise."

The joke served its purpose – it made her feel better. "I don't think there are any along the way to worry about, Mr. Cooke." She wanted to call him by his first name, but wasn't sure it would be proper.

His face split in a great, glorious warm smile that sent Sadie's heart into a backflip. "We really should go. Their house is on the other side of town." He looked at the woman in his arms, who now had her head against his shoulder, her eyes closed. She hadn't put up a fuss when he picked her up – all her strength was spent for the moment.

They left the shack and headed back to the Wallers'. Sadie walked beside Harrison, watching her mother for signs of discomfort. Or worse – her body was so still, she almost looked like she had died after he picked her up. But Sadie could hear her moan softly now and then, confirming that she was still quite alive.

Sadie was glad he'd taken the initiative and gathered her up. She had previously planned to support her mother and walk back to the house with her, or even walk back by herself and ask if she could borrow the Wallers' wagon. This was much quicker. She smiled at him gratefully.

"In the street there! What are you about?" a woman's voice called.

Sadie turned toward the sound. A plump woman stood on the porch of the mercantile, looking perturbed. *Dunnigan's* was painted on a small board that hung above her head by the door.

Doc Waller stopped. "Good morning, Mrs. Dunnigan! Afraid I can't talk – got sickness to tend to!" He trotted to catch up with his wife and Harrison, who hadn't slowed for a second.

"You there – young lady! What are you doing with her? Is she dead?" The woman actually sounded hopeful.

Anger ignited within Sadie. "She most certainly is not! In fact, I plan on seeing she makes a full recovery!" She turned back before she said something harsh, and pointedly ignored the huffing and puffing of the woman launching herself off the porch and following them.

They reached the Wallers' house and quickly went inside. Mrs. Dunnigan shoved her way in before Sadie could shut the door. "Why has that woman been brought here? No decent Christian would be caught dead touching such a disgusting creature!"

Sadie spun to face her. "How dare you! She's sick, and the doctor is going to treat her! No *decent* Christian would do less!"

Harrison was already following Doc Waller upstairs. He slowed at the exchange, but Grandma Waller appeared at the top of the stairs and quickly motioned him up. Sadie watched as he reluctantly continued.

"I don't know who you are, young lady, but you have no idea what you've done, bringing that woman into this house! Not to mention that Cooke boy – what's he doing hauling her about?"

Sadie bit her tongue to stay civil. It worked, but only partly. "I can only conclude by your obvious disdain for my mother that you are disgusted to even be in her presence. That being the case, I strongly suggest you leave." That wasn't so bad, considering how angry she felt. She opened the door for the woman, her jaw set and chin high.

Mrs. Dunnigan's mouth dropped open. "Your *mother*?! Well, I might have known, the way your hair is loose like a strumpet's! Like mother, like daughter, I always say!"

Sadie's hand had just balled itself into a fist, with the intention of burying it in Mrs. Dunnigan's haughty face, when Harrison rushed down the stairs. "Leaving so soon, Mrs. Dunnigan? Well then, may I escort you back to the mercantile? Those *outlaws* are still at large, you know."

Mrs. Dunnigan looked like she was going to let him have it with both barrels – until the word outlaws registered on her consciousness. Her eyes widened and she quickly looked to the door. "You can come back with me, and pay your pa's bill." She turned to Harrison in a huff. "It's overdue. I'll not sell you another thing until it's paid in full."

"By all means! Shall we?" Harrison motioned for her to precede him and she stomped across the front porch and into the street. He winked at Sadie as he walked past. "I'll return shortly. Thank you for not striking her, no matter how much she deserved it." He then stopped on the threshold, turned and whispered. "And your hair makes you look like a magical fairy princess. Never let that old hag tell you otherwise." He smiled the same warm smile as before, gave a small bow, and headed out the door.

Mrs. Dunnigan huffed, puffed and snuffed all the way back to the mercantile. Harrison followed along, his jaw tight. The old bat had really gone too far this time. Her hatred of anything sinful – which, in her mind, was anything not to her standards – got on most people's nerves. But most people had credit at the mercantile and appeased her in order to survive. Thankfully, he had money with him, and, if he was lucky, it was enough to pay his stepfather's bill.

He would have to explain to Miss Jones about Mrs. Dunnigan's view of the world and how she was, of course, the only decent upstanding citizen in it. Though Miss Jones had probably figured it out already.

Mrs. Dunnigan waddled behind the counter and pulled out a cigar box. She sifted through varying bundles of receipts until she found the one she wanted.

"Twenty dollars and seventeen cents! I'll not take a penny less!"

"Has anyone ever told you how lovely your skin looks when you're collecting money, Mrs. Dunnigan?" He shouldn't have said it, but her treatment of Miss Jones gnawed at him.

Mrs. Dunnigan's eyes narrowed. "Was that an insult?"

"Of course not!" he replied, pretending to be affronted. He reached into his pocket and pulled out the money. A good thing he'd been able to sell some livestock that week. He counted out the amount and handed it to her.

She took it, shoved it into another box, and then handed him the bundle of receipts, never once taking her eyes off him.

He took the receipts from her and turned to leave.

"You no longer have credit with me, Harrison Cooke. You and that pack of filth can pay cash from now on."

Harrison turned back and studied her. He'd never seen her so riled up before, and made sure not to join her in high dudgeon. "Tell me, Mrs. Dunnigan … what makes a woman like you hate God's creation so very, very much?"

She started at the question, truly taken aback for a moment, then squared her shoulders. "I don't hate God's creation – only the disgusting filth in it. Like that woman you toted over to Doc Waller's house. She's better off dead. Then maybe this town can start to grow and some decent folks will settle here."

"But there are decent folks who've settled here, aren't there?" His voice was calm, level, but he was keeping it so with an effort.

"Decent? Like you, I suppose – a dirty pig farmer without a penny to his name? Your thieving brothers in prison? Your mother dead not a year on account of your pa's drinking? Decent? The apple doesn't fall far from the tree! Don't tell me folks here are decent! They're no better than you are!"

Harrison should have been angry, but all he felt for her now was pity. What could have happened to make her this way? "You are, of course, entitled to your opinion, Mrs. Dunnigan. But your opinion is just that. It doesn't make you right. Scripture says that we are all created in

God's image – even myself, even my stepfather, even Teresa ... and even you. And if I hear you disparage God's image again as you did at Doc Waller's, I assure you that an extension of credit will be the least of your worries." He paused to let that sink in. "Good day." He tipped his hat and left.

He walked quickly back to the house. Mean spirited as she was, Mrs. Dunnigan would hold to her threat of not allowing his family any more store credit. He'd have to make sure he had the cash to work with when he needed supplies – which, unfortunately, would be later that day. But before that, he needed to take care of Miss Jones and her mother – he wanted to get them settled before he headed back to the farm.

And meanwhile, there was the issue of his brothers' pardons. He had to find out what was in that letter – for all he knew, they had already been released and were on their way home, or the pleas had been rejected and he needed to find more evidence. But he had his suspicions about where to look ...

As it turned out, when he got back to the Wallers', there wasn't much settling left to do. Dr. Waller had agreed to let the two women stay there for the time being. He was going to have his hands full nursing Miss Menendez back to health, so he asked Harrison to contact Miss Jones's family, and Harrison agreed.

He entered the extra bedroom Grandma Waller had prepared, stood quietly and took in the sight of mother and daughter as the doctor pulled the curtains shut to help keep the room warm.

Teresa Menendez was propped against several pillows, and looked better already just from getting out of the weather. Miss Jones sat in a rocking chair at one side of the bed, with Grandma Waller on the other attempting to spoon broth into the sick woman's mouth. "It'll make you feel better, dear. You haven't had a thing in days. It's a miracle you haven't starved to death!"

Teresa looked at the spoon in front of her, then around the room. "I … I can't pay you," she began, her bottom lip trembling. "I don't have money."

Miss Jones left the chair and sat beside her on the bed. "You don't have to worry about a thing. You won't need money ever again, I'll see to that. Just concentrate on getting well. Now have some broth. It will warm you up."

Teresa's eyes locked with her daughter's. "Who are you again?"

"I'm your daughter," came out a whisper.

"I have … a daughter?"

A single tear blazed a trail down Miss Jones's left cheek. It nearly tore Harrison's heart out. "Yes, of course you have a daughter, and she's here to take care of you."

The woman again looked around. "This sure is a … a fine room. I'm not dead, am I?"

Miss Jones gently hugged her. "No, Mama, you're not dead."

Teresa's eyes widened. "You …" she began then coughed. "You called me 'Mama'. If'n I'm your mama, then who's your papa?"

"Horatio Jones."

"Oh my …" Teresa's eyes grew even larger just before they rolled upwards. She fell against the pillows in a dead faint. Everyone looked on in shock.

Dr. Waller waved Miss Jones off the bed and began to examine Teresa. After a moment, he turned to her. "Does the mention of your father always have such an effect on women?"

Miss Jones rolled her own eyes at the lame joke. "She must have remembered."

"Just what happened between your ma and pa, child?" Grandma Waller asked.

"Well ... that's what I hope to find out."

And Harrison silently vowed to help, especially if it meant getting to find out more about the lovely Miss Jones.

SIX

Nearly a week passed. Harrison Cooke still had no word from the sheriff. And neither Harrison, nor Sadie, nor the Wallers had had much word from Sadie's mother. She'd hardly spoken to anyone since the mention of Horatio Jones.

Sadie had sat with her several times a day at first, but eventually left her alone at Doc Waller's suggestion. Her mother slept most of the time anyway, which she desperately needed for her recovery. But Sadie needed to make her understand that everything would be all right, that she wouldn't have to worry about taking care of herself ever again. She couldn't stand the look of distrust in her mother's eyes, even though she understood where it came from.

"Give her time, dear – she'll come around once she feels better." Grandma Waller took a loaf of bread out of the oven and set it on the table. "It must be quite a shock to have your child suddenly turn up after eighteen years. Hand me those pies, will you?"

"Sure, Grandma." Sadie had taken to calling her "Grandma," just like everyone else in town. She handed her the apple pies one at a time. They had been baking bread all morning, and the pies would take up the afternoon. It felt nice to work in the kitchen with Grandma.

It was even nicer to know the meal being prepared today was special. Mr. Cooke was coming to supper. Sadie felt herself blush at the mere thought of him. He'd been over every day, twice a day, to see them, but never stayed longer than was proper – and never stayed to eat. Today was a first.

She absentmindedly smoothed her dress. Mr. Cooke – correction, *Harrison* (Grandma had them on a first-name basis) had brought her trunk the second day of her stay. She wanted to look nice for him and had ironed her best blue calico.

"I know she must be thinking about things. A lot of things," Sadie replied to distract herself from thoughts of the soon-to-arrive guest.

"Of course she is, child. Good heavens, it's a lot of regret to have to wrestle with. And she's doing it alone. Most folks don't come out of a fight like that, but I have a feeling your mother will."

"I know she will."

Grandma smiled. "I suspect the good Lord is having a word or two with her. She asked for a Bible the other day, so I gave her mine."

"Yes, I noticed it on the bedside table. Thank you. In fact … thank you for everything. I promise to repay you for all your kindness. You've gone far beyond what a lot of people would do."

"Hush, now – almost anyone in town would do the same. Besides, there's no hotel in town yet. Where else would you stay?"

They both laughed, but for only a moment. Sadie suddenly sobered. "I know one person who wouldn't show the same generosity."

Grandma's face soured. "Irene Dunnigan. Now there's someone who needs either a good dose of Christian charity or a good knock on the head. Or maybe both."

"Maybe we ought to let Harrison have a go at her?"

Grandma looked shocked for a moment before she burst into laughter. "I hope you haven't brought that tree incident up again! Leave it be, child – the man has his pride, after all."

Sadie smiled. She'd been teasing Harrison all week about it. "I don't know … it might do Mrs. Dunnigan some good."

Grandma snorted. "You can't let things get to you like that. You've got to be strong. Especially out here in this wilderness."

"What do you mean?"

"What I mean, child, is that Mrs. Dunnigan let something get the best of her years ago, and now look at her. She's a bitter old woman who hates the world, and hates herself even more."

"What happened?"

"Well …" Grandma Waller seemed to be having an internal debate. "Aw, after how she treated you and your mama, you have a right to know. But most folks don't know this, and I'm not one to get wrapped up in gossip, so this doesn't leave this room."

"I understand."

"Okay. To hear her husband Wilfred tell it, Irene's pa got into gambling, drinking and women. Ruined the family. Killed himself besides – he got himself shot in a poker game back in Iowa. The mother couldn't cope, and she drank some poison and killed herself, leaving poor Irene behind. All that drove Irene a little crazy, Wilfred says."

Sadie poured them both a cup of coffee. "How did they end up out here?"

"Wilfred was betrothed to Irene by then," Grandma began as they sat with their cups. "Married her to please his family and, at her urging, came out west. She didn't want to stay in Iowa, not when she had so many bad memories of the place."

Sadie sighed. No wonder Mrs. Dunnigan was so venomous toward her mother. "She hates anyone having to do with the vices that dragged her father down."

"Yes, she does. But she compounds it by condemning everyone around her, and always having to get the last word. Lord knows we've all prayed for her. But she's the one who has to want to change."

"I know what … *cough* … what you mean." Sadie and Grandma turned to find Teresa standing in the doorway. "Is that coffee? I'd sure like some," she rasped.

"Mama," Sadie whispered. "Of course! Come, come sit with us." She got up and pulled a chair out for her mother, who sat carefully, still weak.

"Look at you all up and about!" Grandma said as she got up and busied herself at the stove. "But you best not stay down here long – you do still need your rest." She stirred the pot of stew she'd made for supper, poured Teresa a cup of coffee, and then refilled the other cups. The three women sat silently for a few moments, the only sound the occasional pop from the fire in the cookstove.

Teresa finally spoke. "I wasn't always the kind of woman I am now." She stared straight ahead, her cup in her hands, and took a slow sip. "I was a respectable girl. Just like you." She nodded to Sadie.

Sadie had to fight to keep quiet. She wanted to tell her mother it didn't matter, that her old life was behind her now, that she could start over. But letting her speak was more important.

"I was betrothed to a man that I hated. My father had arranged it – he was one of Papa's business partners in Monterrey, where we lived. He was a good thirty years older than I was, and rich." Teresa snorted in disgust. "Oh, he was plenty rich. But I didn't care. I refused to marry a man I cared nothing about, and who repulsed me."

Sadie closed her eyes at the words. How could anyone do that to a child? "Did your father want you to marry him just because he was a wealthy man?"

Teresa held her cup to her lips again, "Yes." She took another sip. "I had to do something. But I wasn't brave enough to run away. So I did the only thing I could think of – I found another man."

"My father?"

"I figured if I was already married, my folks couldn't make me marry someone else. But I went about it all wrong." She looked at Sadie, tears in her eyes. "I'm so sorry ... so very sorry."

"What did you do?" Sadie asked in a whisper.

"I had to get married quick. I figured – fool that I was – that if I got pregnant, the man would have to marry me. But I was wrong."

"What are you saying?" Sadie asked, though she already had a guess.

"I ran. I ran all the way out of the state, all the way to Paso del Norte. And when I got there, I met – and seduced – your father. And my plan worked … except for the part where he married me. By the time I knew I was expecting, he'd gone back to his ranch. I never saw him again."

Sadie took the cup from her mother's hands and held them. They were very cold, and she rubbed them as she spoke. "I don't care what happened – I'm just glad I found you. Someone here in Clear Creek sent word you were sick. I had to come."

Teresa smiled, and then began coughing.

Grandma immediately got up and went around the table. She rubbed Teresa's back before she helped her out of the chair. "Best get you back to bed."

Teresa stopped her and turned to Sadie. "Miss Bess. She must've done it before they got chased out of town." She began to cough again.

"No argument this time," Grandma said sternly. "Back upstairs you go."

A knock suddenly sounded at the door.

Sadie got up, but instead of answering the door, she went to her mother and hugged her. "I love you."

Grandma let go, and her lower lip quivered as she watched mother and daughter hold each other at last. "I'll just ... go get the door. It's probably Harrison."

As soon as Grandma was gone, Teresa weakly pulled back. "Don't make the sort of mistakes I've made. Promise me you won't. You're the only right thing I've ever done."

"I promise, Mama," Sadie said as her tears began to fall, unable to hold them back.

"Promise me you'll marry a man who truly loves you."

Sadie sniffed and nodded. "If I ever find one, I will."

"One may be closer than you think. You see him, you go get him." Her coughing started again. Sadie pulled her back into her arms.

Harrison and Grandma entered the kitchen. "Miss Menendez! So good to see you out of … bed." Harrison said, slowing as her hacking interrupted him. He pulled a clean handkerchief out of his jacket pocket and handed it to her. She took it gratefully and held it to her mouth.

"I was just taking her upstairs," Sadie said as she guided her mother toward the hall. "If you could excuse us for a moment?"

"By all means. I'm glad you're beginning to feel better, Miss Menendez."

Her coughing stilled, she nodded and let Sadie lead her up the stairs. Once in the bedroom, Sadie hugged her again before helping her into bed.

"That young man down there … he has taken a liking to you."

Sadie pulled a quilt over her. "Nonsense, Mama. He's just … just looking out for us while we're here."

"Mark my words, girl – he is not 'just looking out' for you. Trust me, I can tell the difference between a man who just lusts after a woman, and one who actually feels something."

Sadie tucked the quilt around her and smiled. If only her words were true. Though even if they were, what did it matter? It wasn't as if she'd completely set her cap for him. Or had she? He *was* very attractive. Yes, that was probably it – she was just a little lonesome and attracted to him. Besides, as soon as her father found them, both she and her mother would be gone, whisked away across the Oregon Territory to home. "You get some rest, Mama. I'll bring you something to eat later." She kissed her mother on the forehead and left the room.

But as she descended the stairs, she began to wonder. Would her father even allow her to marry a poor, dirty pig farmer in a nothing town in the middle of the prairie? Before she got halfway down the stairs she knew the answer – Horatio Jones would never let the heiress of his ever-growing cattle empire marry a dirt-poor anything. No matter how well mannered he was. It just wasn't done.

Harrison sat in the parlor and held his hat in his hands. He'd worn his Sunday best, but wasn't sure it was good enough. The trousers were too short, the jacket patched at the elbows, and it had taken a good while to find the tie; it was in the barn, of all places, being used to hold a bridle together. He suspected his stepbrothers had something to do with it. They often did. He would've found the tie sooner, but it really had been a long time since he'd had a reason to wear his Sunday best ...

Well, now wasn't the time to worry about it. He had more important matters on his mind, one in particular. And he wished she would hurry up and come downstairs.

"Now, Harrison Cooke – if I didn't know any better, I'd say you were nervous."

Harrison turned to see Grandma Waller smirking down at him. "Not at all, I assure you," he replied, then caught himself twisting his hat in his hands.

Grandma nodded knowingly. "I'll just take that hat ... before you tear it up." She held out her hand.

He returned her stare boldly. But he also handed her the hat.

"That's better. And I hope you like apple pie. There's a little lady upstairs who fussed for hours over the baking ... once she found out we were having a guest." Grandma winked and left.

Harrison suppressed a smile and wiped his hands on his trousers. Perhaps Sadie Jones felt something more than gratitude toward him. It would certainly make the afternoon go more smoothly. He was nervous enough with what he'd planned, and didn't want any interruptions when it came time to speak with her.

Blast it, why were his hands so sweaty?

He took a deep breath. This must be what it feels like to ask a girl to marry you. But he wasn't going to ask for Sadie's hand in marriage, though the thought had entered his mind earlier and stuck there. No, this was something else, something that would help all of them. And he was positive she would be pleased with his proposal ...

"Harrison, I hope you didn't mind waiting," Sadie said as she entered the parlor. "Doc isn't home yet, but as soon as he gets here we'll eat."

"That's quite all right. I came early because I wanted to discuss something with you."

"Oh?"

He nodded, unable to speak. Good Lord, but she was beautiful. Her eyes were brightened by the afternoon sun shining in through the lace-curtained window. She wore a beautiful blue dress and had braided her long hair and wrapped it around her head like a dark, glistening crown. Her apron was fresh and white with a spot of something here and there, probably cinnamon from the pies he could smell baking in the oven.

Harrison swallowed hard and resisted the urge to wipe his hands on his trousers again. The thought of marriage suddenly unstuck itself and raced to the forefront of his mind. If she were his wife, he'd never let her out of his sight.

Which brought him to the matter at hand. "I know you will need to be returning home. Your family must be worried sick about you, and there's been no word from the sheriff since he took off after the outlaws almost two weeks ago. He's determined to catch the men responsible for the stage robbery, but I dare say he likely doesn't even know you were abducted. But outlaws have struck in these parts before, and I imagine the sheriff suspects they are one and the same gang."

"I suppose they could be. But what did you wish to discuss?"

"I wish to offer my services as escort for you and your mother."

"Escort?"

"Protection."

"Protection … from what?"

"The outlaws, of course. I wish to escort you home."

Sadie's eyes widened. She opened her mouth to speak but nothing came out. If Harrison didn't know any better, she looked like she wanted to say something that shouldn't be spoken in polite company. He'd seen that same look on his mother's face upon occasion. And so what she did next, he assumed any lady would do.

She fled from the room.

SEVEN

Sadie retreated to the kitchen, which thankfully was empty. Grandma must have gone upstairs to check on her mother. She absently took the lid from the stew pot and gave the contents a stir.

Why in Heaven's name was she so upset? Harrison had only offered to take her back to her ranch. Her home. Her father … all right, she admitted, that part was upsetting. It would mean seeing her father sooner than expected.

And parting from Harrison sooner than she wanted. She did so enjoy his company, and had come to know him better over the last week. His descriptions of the English countryside fascinated her, and she loved to hear him talk of London and his family there. But she dared not let herself feel anything for him – her mother was more important, and she still had to convince her father to let her come live with them at the ranch. She would *not* leave her behind in Clear Creek!

She stirred the stew one last time and checked on the pies before returning to the parlor. Harrison stood as she entered, confusion on his face. "I ... I thought I smelled supper burning," she stammered. "And I needed to check on dessert."

Harrison's face broke into a warm smile. "Oh, of course. It all smells wonderful, by the way. Come, do sit down."

She went to the settee and sat. He joined her and they enjoyed a companionable silence for a few moments.

"Sadie ..." Harrison's whisper was deep and throaty.

She looked at him and swallowed.

He cleared his throat and scooted closer. "I don't wish to frighten you, but you do need a man's protection out here. I rescued you, and I feel I am responsible for you until your father comes. If he does not come to fetch you, it could mean that he fell victim to the outlaws as well."

Sadie shook her head. "No ..."

"I'm sorry if that upsets you, but if he doesn't come soon then I feel it's my duty to see you home." He turned to the window, moved a lace curtain aside, and looked out to the street. "You cannot plan to stay here forever."

Forever. The word seemed to hang over them. Sadie had never thought about where she would spend the rest of her life, or with whom … until now. She studied him as he continued to look out at the street. A wagon rolled by, and his eyes latched onto the horse being pulled along behind it.

He was so different from the other men she was familiar with. His looks were striking, of course, but she'd met handsome men before. No, Harrison Cooke had something the others didn't. It was a quiet strength, wrapped up in polite manners. His English mother had no doubt taken her job of teaching her sons proper deportment very seriously. It was hard to imagine his brothers being falsely accused and locked in prison.

But at the same time, she knew these men wouldn't hesitate to do what was necessary to protect her. This was not some fancy English fop she'd read about in a novel. This was a man who'd spent the last eight years taming the Oregon prairie with other men of his ilk, pioneers who wanted a better life and were willing to pay the price to get it.

"I have no doubt my father will turn up eventually. Until that time, I plan to take care of my mother and see that she gets well."

Finally he turned back to her. His eyes focused on her mouth, and he swallowed hard. "I shall continue to look after you, then. And check daily on you both."

Sadie's stomach did its little flip. Only this time it was more of a flop, as something seemed to sink deep into her. When she finally recovered from the odd sensation, she found herself staring at Harrison's mouth with the same intensity he stared at hers.

"Erm, sorry to interrupt ..."

Sadie had to fight to tear her gaze away. That felt even stranger.

Doc stood out in the hallway. "Is supper about ready?"

Sadie glanced back at Harrison, and realized they had been leaning toward one another. To Doc Waller, it must have looked like they were about to kiss.

"Well, it sure smells good! I think I'll just go see what's in the oven." Doc chuckled and turned to head down the hall.

Sadie swallowed as she watched him leave. Why couldn't she speak? What was wrong with her? Did she *want* Harrison to kiss her?

She turned to him again, and again his eyes immediately darted to her mouth. Yes … yes, she did – and apparently he had the same idea. But what should she do?

You see him, you get him, her mother's words echoed in her mind. But how could she? What if he only wanted to kiss her because she was the one eligible woman in town *to* kiss? She'd seen how the other men stared at her when she went out with Grandma to run errands over the last few days. Harrison had warned her not to leave the house unescorted, and she'd soon found out why. And Doc Waller had mentioned he suddenly had a lot more men coming to be tended since she'd arrived. Was Harrison different, or, like all the others, simply in desperate want of a female?

Well, probably not quite like the others – he'd never even *met* "Tantalizing Teresa."Or so he'd said …

His gaze was still locked on her face. "What's ... for supper?" he asked as if in a daze.

"I don't remember," she sighed, her mouth now inches from his. He had one arm across the back of the settee, the other hand coming up under her chin as she stared at him. When he took her chin in his hand and tilted her face up, she thought she might faint. His fingers were warm, his breath on her face even warmer.

He bent his face to hers, and it was as if he was swallowing her up. "You have my protection, Miss Jones," he whispered. "But ..."

"But what?" she whimpered.

"But ..." Suddenly he pulled away, his eyes downcast. "But I don't know how much longer I can protect you from myself." And like a proper gentleman, he stood to his feet and, clearly abashed, left the room.

Sadie was left staring after him, in shock at his abrupt departure. She hadn't wanted him to go. But, thinking about how she had broken and run for the kitchen just a few minutes before, she understood. And slowly, she smiled.

No, Harrison Cooke certainly wasn't like the other men.

Harrison rushed into the kitchen so fast he nearly knocked Doc over. "Blazes, boy! What's the trouble? The house on fire?" He watched Harrison glance down the hall toward the parlor, and nodded in understanding. "Oh, I see. The house isn't on fire, but you sure are!"

"Dr. Waller, please …"

"Did you kiss her?"

Harrison straightened. "Good Heavens, no!"

Doc slammed the lid back on the stewpot, from which he'd been sneaking a bite. "Well, why not? What's the matter with you? The prettiest girl around for fifty miles and you're telling me you don't want to kiss her?"

"Please, she'll hear you …"

"Well, I should hope."

"Kissing her would have been a, a, a travesty."

"A what?"

"A mistake."

Doc stared at him a moment. Then they both heard the sound of Sadie squeaking in outrage and stomping up the stairs, followed by a door slamming.

"Well, you can bet she heard that," Doc scolded.

Harrison sank heavily into the nearest chair. "It's not that I didn't wish to. But I ... I don't want her to get the wrong impression."

"Son, this isn't London – this is Clear Creek. Eligible young women aren't just scarce – until last week they were non-existent. I'm telling you right now, if you fancy that little lady, you'd best stake a claim to her before someone else does."

"But when her father comes ..."

"... then we'll deal with her father," Doc finished. "I saw my Sarah for the first time and two weeks later we were married. And that was in Philadelphia, which isn't exactly the back of the beyond. After we settled in Kansas, I brought more than my share of babies into the world, a lot of which came out west with us. Those folks went on to Oregon City, and most of them are probably married by now. But in Clear Creek, what are your chances of finding a woman to wed?"

Slim indeed, Harrison thought, and not for the first time.

"And the good Lord saw fit to drop one right in front of you. Don't you think you owe Him at least the courtesy of accepting the gift?"

Harrison felt like a cad. He'd wanted to kiss her all right – kiss her until she swooned. But he wanted more time with her, and he'd thought that escorting her back to her ranch with a few of the sheriff's men would give him that time. Not to mention, now that he thought of it, it would give him time to think of a good reason Mr. Jones should let him marry her. And furthermore, Mrs. Dunnigan had the town thinking Sadie was no better than her mother. He'd like more time for the old biddy's tempest-in-a-teapot to blow over.

Dr. Waller was right – if he wanted her, he needed to do something about it. But there were so many obstacles: his wastrel stepfather and stepbrothers, his concern that he wouldn't be able to provide for her in the manner to which she was no doubt accustomed, Mrs. Dunnigan's great fat mouth.

But first he had to deal with his current dilemma – that after his *faux pas* in the kitchen, she probably thought he didn't care a whit about her. Or worse, that he just wanted her body. He did want it, mind you, but with a wedding ring attached and her heart committed to his. He would simply have to explain it to her. In fact, he ought to march up there right now and do so!

Doc saw the steel in his eye, and grinned. "That's it, son – go get her. Keep those fancy manners your mama taught you, but don't let them spoil a good thing. She'll be more of a mind to let you court her if she knows how you feel."

"Court her? What happened to 'staking claim'?"

"All women want to be courted a least a little. Even out here."

"I wouldn't know about that – I have yet to see anyone get married out here."

Doc laughed as Grandma walked in. "What's going on? Sadie's upstairs mad as a rattler. Harrison, what did you do?"

"A misunderstanding, which I will be correcting shortly." He marched down the hall to the stairs. But just as he was about to set foot on the first step, Mr. Mulligan burst through the door. "Doc, Harrison!

The sheriff's back! And he's got one of them outlaws!"

Sadie sat on Doc and Grandma's bed. She'd been sleeping on a pallet in her mother's room, but didn't want to disturb her. Instead, she'd walked in on Grandma – and then had to apologize for slamming the door. Now that Grandma was downstairs, she let the tears fall.

First, Harrison acted like he was clearly attracted to her, and just wanted to be gentlemanly about it. A minute later, he called the possibility of kissing her "a travesty." What sense was she supposed to make of that?!

Maybe she and her mother were becoming a burden for him. He was coming by twice a day, and she couldn't imagine how he managed that and worked on his farm too. Maybe she was confusing him by her presence. She was certainly becoming a temptation for him, and she didn't want to do that.

She didn't want to be just an appetizing morsel waiting to be eaten, the way men had treated her mother. And around here, if Mrs. Dunnigan had her way, that's the way everyone would see her. Harrison's desire to protect her was flattering, but he also seemed desperate to get her out of town. Perhaps the temptation was too much.

Sadie went over their conversation again in her head. His resolve to protect her body was admirable, but what about her heart? She sighed – that was something she should have seen to herself. She hadn't realized until that afternoon that her heart had allowed the Englishman in. Worse still, she didn't know how to get him out.

There was a logical solution, however – pack up her mother as soon as she was able, and leave town. She'd gotten herself out here, albeit with a little help from Harrison, and she could get back. Surely someone here could contact her father and see she was returned safely.

She didn't want Harrison to have to escort her across miles of prairie in order to rid himself of the temptation she represented; she'd already done enough damage. What if he couldn't hold out? What if *she* couldn't? Until that day, she'd never felt this way around a man, never had an inner longing pull at the deepest part of her soul when she was with one. What *was* it? Was this what it felt like to fall in love?

If so, they could keep it, thank you very much indeed!

Sadie wiped her tears. She wanted a man to marry her because he loved her, not because he needed to use her body to slake his lust. And if Harrison wasn't even sure which he felt, it was probably better to not befuddle him further …

A commotion downstairs interrupted her thoughts. She stood just as Grandma burst back into the room. "The sheriff's back! He'll want to see you – he and the posse managed to bring back one of those no-good outlaws!"

Sadie's eyes widened, and cold slipped up her spine. Which one could it be? And would she be able to identify him? They were wearing masks the entire time she'd been in their company.

"Best get your coat. Supper will have to wait until after you've talked with the sheriff. Harrison'll take you."

Sadie nodded numbly as she left the room, went downstairs and donned her coat.

Harrison came out of the kitchen, where he'd been speaking with Doc Waller and another gentleman. "Are you all right?" he asked.

She looked up at him. His face was full of concern.

Without warning he pulled her into his arms and held her tight. "I'll be right there – you have nothing to fear. They only want to know if the scoundrel is one of the men who seized you."

"Thank you," she gasped. His embrace was like Heaven: warm, strong, safe. His voice was a soothing balm, wondrous. If she was still intent on leaving, it was going to be harder than she thought.

Harrison pulled away just enough to take her hand and lead her from the house. Once outside – ever the gentleman! – he offered her his arm. She took it, and they made their way to the sheriff's office.

Sadie had never seen Clear Creek so lively – half the town must've been part of the posse. Horses were tethered outside the sheriff's office and Mulligan's saloon across the street. She saw more people in several minutes than she'd seen the entire previous week. Mrs. Dunnigan was charging around, yelling about wanting to see "the criminal" and brandishing a hatchet. Apparently the outlaws had caused quite a few problems for the townsfolk, and everyone wanted a piece of their hides.

Sadie didn't feel one bit sorry for the man.

"Go on home, everyone!" The sheriff was tall, middle-aged and kindly-looking, even as he hollered at the closest Clear Creek could come to a crowd. "We'll let you folks know, just as soon as we find out anything."

"Find out if them's the ones that stole my cows!" a voice yelled.

"And mine!"

"What about the stage robbery?"

"Folks, we just got back – me and the boys need a rest. Then we'll find out if this fellow is connected to any of your missing livestock."

"You mean you're not going to do anything?" Mrs. Dunnigan huffed as she shoved her way forward.

The sheriff sighed and rolled his eyes. "Good afternoon, Mrs. Dunnigan."

"Don't you 'good afternoon' me! Is this one of the outlaws or not?"

"That's what I hope to find out. We need to question him, and gather evidence."

"Evidence? What evidence? There are only so many people in town! I would think process of elimination would be sufficient!"

"Mrs. Dunnigan, we still need proof. You can't go accusing folks of being outlaws without proof."

"What about a witness?" Harrison called out as he led Sadie to the front.

"Now who do you have there, Harrison?" the sheriff asked.

"Miss Sadie Jones. The passenger the highwaymen abducted when they robbed the stage."

Mrs. Dunnigan gasped. The rest of the crowd whispered amongst themselves.

And two figures silently backed away and slipped out of sight. If this so-called witness could identify the captured outlaw, she might be able to identify them as well.

EIGHT

"Abducted?" the sheriff exclaimed. "She's the missing passenger? But I thought she made her way into town on her own. One of the boys told me when they brought us supplies a few days ago."

Harrison drew Sadie against him. Mrs. Dunnigan snorted disgustedly behind them, which he ignored. "No, sir. I left to meet the stage on account of some mail I was expecting. When the stage didn't arrive, I went searching for it, and discovered it had been robbed. I took care of the wounded driver, then followed the outlaws' trail in the snow to a cabin north of the first ridge." He looked at Sadie with the same concern as before, and her insides melted like fresh-churned butter. "Thank the Lord, it also snowed during our escape, and made it much harder for them to track us."

The sheriff looked, open-mouthed, from Sadie to Harrison and back again. "Is this true?"

"Yes, sir," Sadie replied. "The stage was held up where the road forks. Four outlaws took the strongbox, the mailbag, and me. We rode for hours to a cabin, just as Harrison said."

The sheriff took off his hat and slapped his leg with it. "Well, I'll be hornswoggled. How did you manage to get away?"

Harrison blushed and went silent. Sadie looked at him and nudged him gently.

"Well?" the sheriff urged.

Harrison sighed. "I performed a few … animal calls."

"Animal calls?"

Raucous laughter erupted from some men in the crowd. "Did you scare 'em off imitatin' a hoot owl?" a man shouted.

Harrison's pride was pricked, and right then and there he did a wolf howl, one good enough to silence his erstwhile critics.

Sadie was also impressed. "That was awfully good," she said, smiling in gratitude at his inventiveness. She didn't really care if he had mimicked one of his pigs; it had gotten her free of the outlaws.

He looked at Sadie and blushed again. "It seems a silly talent to have. But I've been able to imitate animals since I was a child."

"Well, it got the job done, and that's what counts," the sheriff replied. "Come inside, young lady. We need to talk." He turned and went into his office.

Harrison and Sadie moved to follow, but Mrs. Dunnigan grabbed her other arm before she could cross the threshold. "You mean to tell me you were taken by those outlaws and holed up in a cabin with them? Why, the disgrace! No doubt they took their pleasure with you!" She turned to the crowd. "And she nary bats at an eye at the ordeal!"

Several men in the crowd suddenly looked at Sadie like she was a freshly-baked apple – with a worm in it. Mrs. Dunnigan gave a little triumphant smirk.

Harrison was having none of it. He backed out of the door, while at the same time gently coaxing Sadie through it, then shut it behind her. "For your information, Mrs. Dunnigan, I rescued Miss Jones before any such debauchery occurred, which accounts for her surviving the ordeal so admirably. The only disgrace involved seems to be within your own wicked mind. Kindly keep your thoughts to yourself from now on." He turned to go inside.

"Or what?"

Harrison stopped up short. "Pray, dear lady ... or should I say, dear *woman*. Pray you never find out." He turned his back to her and opened the door.

Mrs. Dunnigan was about to retort, but the sheriff's voice from inside was loud, and excited, enough to override her. "Sakes alive – your daddy owns the Big J? He'll be riding in here any day now with guns blazing if he's anything like folks say!" He pushed Harrison out of the way as he hurried onto the porch. "Charlie, Tommy! Get some food and fresh horses – I got a message for you to deliver!"

He spun on his heel to go back inside, but Harrison stopped him. "What's wrong?"

"Nothing's wrong, son! You rescued the daughter of one of the biggest cattlemen in the West! In these parts, that makes her royalty!" He hurried back inside and slammed the door closed behind him.

Harrison stood in shock for a moment. Then he stole a glance at Mrs. Dunnigan, whose jaw hung like a broken gate ... and the opportunity was irresistible. "Well, Mrs. Dunnigan. It seems that the young lady you've been so quick to condemn is the daughter of a king of sorts. A princess, you might say."

The men in the crowd leaned forward and watched the spectacle. They'd never seen Irene Dunnigan at a loss for words before. Her face turned a few shades of red as she noticed the attention now focused on her. With an outraged squeak, she took her hatchet and stomped off toward the mercantile, the crowd breaking into guffaws as she retreated.

"It's all right. He can't hurt you while he's locked up in there," Harrison whispered in her ear from behind her. "Is this one of them?"

His voice calmed her, but Sadie still had to force herself to look at the man sitting in the jail cell. He wasn't wearing a hat, nor a bandana over his lower face – how could she possibly recognize if he had been one of her kidnappers? "I'm not sure."

The man in the cell was reclining on the cot in the cell, smirking. If he recognized her, he certainly gave no indication.

This was terrible. Everyone was counting on her to identify him ... but she'd never seen any of their faces. She turned to Harrison and the sheriff, thinking furiously – and then it came to her. "Make him say something," she whispered.

"What for?" the sheriff whispered back.

"Their faces were covered while I was with them. But they talked in front of me a lot. I might recognize his voice."

The sheriff eyed the outlaw, who eyed him back and then spat. "I don't suppose we can let our new prisoner starve ... you hungry?"

The outlaw's entire demeanor changed. "Now, Sheriff, y'all know I ain't had a thing today! I'm so famished, I can't hardly see straight!"

Sadie tried her best not to let her face show anything to the prisoner. Instead she turned quickly to Harrison and whispered, "I think his name is Cain."

The sheriff overheard her, and nodded at Cain. "Well … I'll see we get you something."

"Much obliged, Sheriff. I ain't worth being accused of nothin' on an empty stomach."

All three looked at Cain, who had no clue he'd just been found out. Harrison took Sadie by the hand and led her to the front office of the jail, with the sheriff right behind.

Once he'd closed the door to the cell area, he sighed in relief. "I can't thank you enough, Miss Jones. I've been after this gang for a long time now. What else can you tell me?"

"I'm sure they called this one Cain. There was another man, Jeb – I think he was the leader. The other two, I have no idea."

"Well, this is a mighty big help, Miss Jones. A couple dozen missing cattle probably don't seem like much to you, but around here it can be life-changing. Folks will be happy to know we caught one of the rustlers, and this'll help us catch up with the rest. I sure hope it's only the one gang."

"Be it one or several, let us hope they don't leave the area before you have a chance to apprehend them," Harrison commented.

"I can agree with that! As soon as the boys and I rest a spell, we'll set out again. The sooner we round up the rest of these good-for-nothings, the better. Your daddy's gonna be mighty proud of you, Miss Jones."

Sadie slumped slightly at the mention of her father.

"I sent word to him, so he should be here within a week at the most. It all depends on where he is now."

Sadie had to sit. She didn't have to worry about Harrison falling into temptation while escorting her across the prairie now. Instead, she had to avoid him until her father arrived, to keep from losing her heart to him – if she hadn't already. She wondered which fate was worse.

Mr. Mulligan poured two shots of whiskey. "Looks like your little brother's a hero."

Jack and Sam Cooke grabbed their shots and slugged them back. Sam growled and slammed his glass on the counter. "Worthless whelp. Now we know why he's been comin' into town so much."

"Sneaky cuss. Wait 'til Pa finds out," Jack added.

"Pa ain't gonna find out nothin'!" Sam snapped. "Last thing we need is fer Pa to ease up on him. Then *we* might have to do some of the work, an' that don't sit well with me."

Mr. Mulligan laughed, poured them each another shot, and moved down the counter to serve his other customers.

Jack leaned into the bar, his head low, his voice lower. "Jeb's gonna kill us."

Sam glanced around before he spoke in the same low tone. "We ain't done nothin' wrong."

"It was Harrison took her from us! What if she recognizes Cain and tells the sheriff? You know that's what's going on 'cross the street right now!"

"Shut up. I can't think with all yer babblin'."

"What happens if'n she sees one of us?"

Sam grabbed him by the collar. "I said, shut up. We'll just have to make sure she doesn't see us, you got that?"

Jack slapped Sam's hand away. "If Jeb finds out she's here, he might cut us out of the deal."

"He can't! It's our deal!"

"You think Jeb cares?" Jack snorted in derision.

Sam growled again. "Well, if he tries to cut our deal, I'll be cuttin' somethin' too – his mangy throat!"

"If'n he don't cut our hearts out first." Jack grabbed his shot and slugged it back.

Sam stared at his own drink and watched the amber liquid swirl as he moved the glass. "Which means we need to cut that girl out, quick-like." He gulped his whiskey down and set the glass on the counter. "Best we figure out a way to get her off by herself."

Now Jack glanced around. Mr. Mulligan was still at the other end of the bar, talking and laughing with several men from the posse. "What about Harrison? He's always in town now. Prob'ly been seein' her this whole time!"

"Just have to make sure he don't get in the way. I'm sure there's all kinds of work Pa wants that boy to do the next few days."

"Nah. He's already done all the work there is to do."

"Not if we make sure he has to do it again," Sam said as he signaled to Mr. Mulligan for another round. The brothers chuckled as the bartender headed their way, whiskey bottle in hand.

NINE

"What do you mean, 'keep an eye out'?" Sadie asked. "Surely the rest of the outlaws wouldn't be foolish enough to come into town, would they?"

"They might wish to free their comrade," Harrison explained. "In which case, now that he's seen *you*, you could well be in danger."

"I don't want to risk it," the sheriff added. "It's best we have someone look after you until your daddy gets here. He'd probably try to hang the whole lot of us if something ever happened to his only daughter."

"But I'm already staying with the Wallers. I'm never alone."

The sheriff shook his head. "They're both getting on in years – neither one would be much help in a shootout. No, I'll have one of my men watch the house."

"I'd like to volunteer, Sheriff. I can see to it Miss Jones is kept safe."

Sadie's eyes widened.

"That's mighty kind of you, Harrison. Can you spare the time away from your farm?"

"I'll make the time. I have no doubt that if the outlaws find Miss Jones is here and has identified their man, they'll come after her." He looked at Sadie. "I can't have that. I'll not see you put in harm's way."

Did he have to look so handsome when he said it? And as his voice dropped in pitch, his eyes looked like hot dark cocoa, a luxury in these parts. How was she supposed to keep from falling for him? His insistence on protecting her didn't help on that score.

Harrison helped her up from the chair and turned to the sheriff. "We must be going. Doc and Grandma have prepared supper for us and are waiting."

"Sure, you go on. I'll finish up here and drop by later this evening – if that's all right, Miss Jones?"

Sadie could only nod. Harrison had already wrapped her arm around one of his and was heading for the door. How did she manage to go from *Surely, I can avoid the man for the next week or so* to Harrison being her self-appointed protector? Although he volunteered for the job, and the sheriff certainly didn't put up any fuss over it. Wasn't it improper for Harrison to be glued to her side? She was sure Mrs. Dunnigan would say so, loudly and at length.

Harrison pulled her along as they went back to the house. "I'll find out who's to take the first watch and how often they plan to change."

"Change?"

"The sheriff won't allow just one man to do the job. They've been looking for these outlaws for weeks. They're tired and hungry, and can only stand watch a few hours at a time. I'll take a shift myself to ensure you're safe for tonight. At some point I can head back to the farm and take care of a few things. And tomorrow, we'll come up with a definite plan for the rest of the week."

Sadie gave him a half smile before she looked away. He looked exceedingly pleased about something, but she couldn't tell what. An hour ago, she was a potential "travesty" and he couldn't wait to get rid of her. Now he couldn't stand to let her out of his sight. Maybe protecting her from the outlaws made it easier for him to protect her from himself. Or something.

They reached the house and went inside. Sadie was delighted to find her mother sitting at the kitchen table with Doc and Grandma. "You're up! Do you feel strong enough to eat with us?"

Teresa took in the sight of Sadie still on Harrison's arm and smiled. "It's why I came down. I'm stronger every day, thanks to you. I only needed a little rest before supper."

Sadie detached herself from Harrison and gave her mother a hug. "I'm so glad!"

Teresa smiled, took one of Sadie's hands and gave it a squeeze.

Grandma got up and began to pull linens from a sideboard. "I'll just go set the table then. We'll eat in the dining room – this is a special occasion, after all. Sadie, you'd best take those pies of yours out of the oven."

"Allow me to help you, Grandma," Harrison offered and followed her into the dining room.

Sadie watched him go. The Wallers' house was modest – a simple dining room and parlor were separated by the center hallway and stairs, with the kitchen in the back and two bedrooms upstairs. It was so much smaller than her father's ranch house, but she loved it and wondered what it would be like to have one of her own someday, especially if it came with a husband and a family.

Harrison ...

Sadie shook herself, and set about taking her pies out of the oven. She placed them to one side to cool before checking the stew. While Grandma and Harrison finished setting the table, she sliced the bread.

Soon the table was ready and the meal laid out upon it. Doc and Grandma beamed as they looked at their guests. Harrison sat at one end of the table, and Doc at the other. Sadie and her mother sat side-by-side, with Grandma opposite them. "We haven't used this table in a long while – the kitchen has been enough for the two of us," Doc said. "But this is much nicer. Harrison, you say the blessing."

When Harrison held both his hands out, Sadie stiffened. She was going to have to hold his hand for the blessing?! She slowly took her mother's hand and stared at the one Harrison offered. He waited, with that same warm smile on his face.

Sadie's mouth went suddenly dry as heat seeped into her bones from some unseen source. She gritted her teeth, took his hand ... and the heat positively exploded.

"Dear Lord, we thank you for this day and those in it. We also thank you for helping our sheriff apprehend one of the outlaws, and pray the others will be taken into custody soon. I thank you for the safety of everyone here. For what we are about to receive, may we be truly thankful." He gave Sadie's hand a squeeze, then looked her right in the eye.

She thought she was going to slide from her chair and into a puddle on the floor. His eyes had a look she'd never seen before – one of determination and strength, as if saying he would not be letting her out of his sight anytime soon. It was so profoundly primal, masculine ... possessive. Even someone as inexperienced as she could recognize it.

Oh, no, she thought. *I'm a dead woman–*

"Sadie! Sadie? Pass the bread, would you?" Grandma requested.

Sadie pulled herself out of her stupor and reached for the plate of bread next to her. Doc chuckled as he began to dish up stew, while her mother patted her leg reassuringly and took a sip of milk.

Apparently she wasn't the only one who'd recognized the look on Harrison's face. And nobody was saying or doing anything to oppose it.

Yep, she was a dead woman, all right ...

After the meal, they took their pie and coffee into the parlor and chatted about the sheriff, the posse and their hunt for the outlaws. Harrison said nothing about a guard being posted, and Sadie figured he didn't want to worry the others.

But even if her mother and Doc were blissfully ignorant of what was happening, Grandma wasn't. Sadie watched as she peeked past the lace curtains to the street for at least the sixth time.

"What in tarnation are you looking at?" Doc finally asked.

"I was just wondering why Henry Fig is sitting across the street twirling his revolver. Boy's been there for the past hour – he should be home having supper with his wife." She turned from the window to Sadie. "Henry's one of the few menfolk around here that has a wife. You'd think he'd rush home to her after being gone more than a week."

"Perhaps he's … waiting to get orders from the sheriff," Harrison offered. "I heard him ask several of the men to stay behind in town and await further instructions."

"Further instructions?" Grandma became irritated. "The only instruction any of those boys wants to hear after all they've been through is 'eat up!' I'd best fix him something – he's looking awful hungry sitting over there."

"I'll help you, Grandma," Sadie said as she stood and began to gather up the dessert plates. Teresa stood also, but Sadie held up a hand. "No, Mama, you stay here unless you'd like to go upstairs. I don't want you to tire."

She smiled and sat. "I think I will sit a while longer before I go up. This has been the nicest day I can remember."

Everyone looked at her, realizing it was true. How many evenings, over how many years, had it been since this woman enjoyed such a simple thing as pie and coffee in a cozy parlor with folks who cared about her? *Probably not since childhood,* Sadie mused. "I'm glad you enjoyed it, because you're going to have this every day!"

Teresa's bottom lip quivered as her tears started.

"Oh, now don't go starting none of that!" Grandma choked out. "I gotta fix something for Henry and take it across the street! Boy'll be wondering who died over here if I hand him a dinner plate all teary-eyed." Everyone laughed as she stomped into the kitchen, wiping her eyes as she went.

Sadie went to a table and picked up a small book. "Here, this will entertain you. It's Grandma's."

"What is it?"

"It's called a 'penny dreadful.' Harrison's mother brought some from England when she came to America, and after she passed Harrison gave them to Grandma. She loves them – they're quite exciting."

Teresa took the little book from her and smiled. "Thank you. For everything."

Sadie bent down to kiss her. "You're welcome," she whispered, then went to the kitchen to help Grandma.

Her mother wasn't the only one who'd enjoyed the pleasure of the afternoon and early evening. In fact, it had bordered on pure bliss for Sadie to watch Harrison joke with Doc, rave about her pies, sip his coffee, and tease Grandma. Somewhere between the praise for her baking and Doc's and Grandma's snorts of laughter, she, despite her valiant efforts not to, had fallen in love.

And she didn't feel like a dead woman anymore either. If anything, she'd never felt more alive.

Sadie couldn't sleep. She tried, for hours, but the realization of her feelings toward Harrison wouldn't leave her be.

She lay on her pallet and listened to her mother's steady breathing. The woman was getting better every day, and sounded better every night. She would be able to make the journey home soon, unless something upset her and she relapsed.

And therein lay the problem. Now Sadie didn't want to go. More specifically, she didn't want to leave Harrison – at least not without letting him have a chance to fall in love with her. Surely he felt something, but the indications were all mixed up. Did he only want her body and not her heart? Was it the other way around? Was he conflicted in some other way?

Sadie groaned and turned over, trying to get comfortable. She was willing to risk it. That look he'd given her before supper … and how he'd always treated her with deference and respect … and how he'd cared for her mother, a fallen woman he'd never even met … well, it all had to add up to something, didn't it? And besides, her heart was no longer her own – the traitorous thing had gone after Harrison despite her plans not to.

Sadie had been a lot of things in her short life, but a coward was not one of them. She would just have to face facts – she was deeply in love with Harrison Cooke.

Okay, then what to do about it? Should she tell him how she felt, and if so, when and how? Or wait it out and see if he made the first move? What if he didn't give an indication of his feelings before her father showed up – press him then or cut the rope? She sighed. Nobody had ever told her that love would be so blasted *complicated* …

Did she hear her mother wheezing? Sadie stilled her own breathing and listened intently. Nope. Not a wheeze, not a cough, nothing.

Sadie let go of the breath she'd been holding. Her mother was on her way to a full recovery. But still, they should probably stay here until she was back to complete health, just to make sure…

BOOM!

Sadie sat up with a start. What was *that*?

A shout from outside suddenly drew her attention, then another.

She looked around. What could be happening? Had the outlaw escaped? She quickly tossed her blankets aside.

There was a sudden rapping on the front door. "Doc! Doc! Mulligan's is on fire!"

Sadie jumped to her feet and reached for her clothes that she'd neatly folded and placed on a chair. She pulled on her blue calico quickly and listened as Doc and

Grandma came out of their room and went downstairs. Teresa groaned and opened one eye. "Go back to sleep, Mama. Nothing to worry about."

"Mm-hm," she mumbled in response, closed her eye, and snuggled deeper into the blankets. Sadie smiled and left the room.

Grandma had gone through the back door of the kitchen and was running to the small barn behind the house. Doc was already heading out the front door with Henry Fig, and Sadie followed them off the front porch and into the street. She stopped and watched the men silhouetted against a bright orange glow, and gasped as the sky itself seemed to come alive with smoke and flame. It was a really *big* fire – Mulligan's saloon was quickly being consumed!

Sadie realized that Grandma must have gone to the barn for buckets or anything else the men could use, and decided she had best help her. But when she turned to run back into the house, a man came out of nowhere and grabbed her. Her yelp of surprise was quickly cut off by a large hand clamped over her mouth. She instinctively bit it, and smiled at the muffled curse of pain, but he stuffed a handkerchief into her mouth before she could cry out.

The man was soon joined by another, who dragged her away from the house toward a couple of horses. She kicked and clawed at them until one grabbed her wrists and lashed them together. The other took the bandana from around his neck and tied it around her head to hold the handkerchief in place.

The bandana smelled atrociously bad – and familiar. *Oh, no ... not again*!

She struggled violently but futilely as a dark cloth sack was yanked over her head. She listened as one man mounted his horse, then nearly lost her breath when she was roughly grabbed and tossed up to him. An arm locked itself around her waist, pinning her against her captor as the dreaded outlaws, once again with Sadie in their clutches, kicked their horses into a gallop and rode as fast as they could out of town.

TEN

Flames shot into the sky as the sheriff and what men were in town tried their best to battle the raging fire. But the fight was in vain. Mulligan's was lost.

Mrs. Mulligan stood across the street in her nightclothes, a shawl wrapped about her shoulders, and bitterly wept. Mr. Mulligan slowly walked across the street to join her once it became apparent the fight was hopeless. He pulled her into his arms and watched as everything they had went up in flames. "It'll be all right, my girl," he whispered against her hair in his soft Irish brogue. "It'll be all right."

Part of the structure caved in on itself and came crashing down. Mrs. Mulligan let out a wail at the sight, and buried her face in her husband's chest.

Mrs. Dunnigan marched down the street toward them. Her husband Wilfred was with the other men, trying to rescue what they could. "Fire cleanses away all sin!" she huffed as she arrived, out of breath.

Mr. Mulligan glared at her. "Don't start, Irene. If you know what's good for you, don't start!"

Surprisingly, Mrs. Dunnigan heeded the warning. "You'll be needing a place to stay while you rebuild. Wilfred and I have plenty of room." She held a hand out to Mrs. Mulligan, who looked at it warily.

Mr. Mulligan stared, his mouth open in shock. "You've always hated our place. Called it a den of iniquity."

"Hated your place. Hated what it did to men. But I never said I didn't like you. Now let me take your wife back to the mercantile where I can fix her a cup of coffee."

Mr. Mulligan hesitated a moment, then gently steered his wife into Mrs. Dunnigan's arms. She, in turn, led her away to help in whatever way she could. And for that, he was grateful. It was easy to forget how folks could come together in a time of crisis. Even Irene Dunnigan. He shook his head in wonderment, then turned back to the fire

Just then, Harrison thundered up on his brother's beautiful black horse Romeo. He reined the steed in and jumped off. "What happened? I could see the fire from the farm! Came as fast as I could!"

"You're too late. It's gone, all gone." Mr. Mulligan sank onto the steps leading up to the sheriff's office.

Doc, the sheriff, and several other men crossed the street and joined them. Doc sat next to Mr. Mulligan. "I'd say you look like a man who could use a drink, but I think you may be out of luck."

Mr. Mulligan couldn't help but chuckle. "All the whiskey in town is gone! Now, when we all could use it the most."

There was no help for it. The rest of the men laughed as well.

"Don't worry, Paddy," the sheriff said. "We'll all help you rebuild. Mulligan's will be back up in no time."

Grandma joined them. "Where's Mrs. Mulligan?"

"Irene took her back to the mercantile. Offered to put us up until we got our place rebuilt."

Everyone looked shocked for a moment before Grandma spoke. "Best enjoy it while you can Mulligan. No offense, Wilfred," she added as she turned to Mr. Dunnigan.

He waved a dismissive hand in the air. "None taken. We'd love to have you stay with us. And I'm sure that, once you have a new place, Irene will be back to her old self."

Some of the men laughed at that as well.

"I've already gotten some lumber in to start work on the hotel," Mr. Van Cleet offered. "You can use what you need."

"And I still got lotsa roofin' shingles from when I put up my barn last fall," another man said.

Harrison smiled. "You've got first pick of my stock this spring!"

Another man offered nails, and several said they'd chip in for a new bar. Frequent customers that they were, they deemed it a sound investment.

Harrison watched with pride as the people of Clear Creek continued to offer materials and the strength of their backs to help Mr. Mulligan rebuild. Sadie should see this. But she must still be at the house, caring for her mother. He turned and looked at the little white house at the other end of town.

In that moment, he knew without a shadow of a doubt he wanted to build a life with Sadie Jones. He could stand it no longer – life was too precious, and too short. He smiled, swung up into the saddle and trotted down the street to tell his prairie princess he loved her, and wanted her to be his wife.

"Didja hafta set fire to Mulligan's, you idjit? What were you thinkin'? It'll take *months* to rebuild!" one of the men wailed.

"I meant to just set the shed on fire, but a dog started barkin' at me! I threw the torch at it to chase it off … but it landed on the whiskey barrels on the back porch …" The other man whined as he held a hand over his fresh black eye. "You didn't hafta wallop me fer it! We got what we wanted, didn't we?"

The first man calmed at the remark and glared at a bound and gagged Sadie as she lay atop a familiar pile of hay. "We shouldn't o' brought her here. Only a matter of time 'fore Harrison comes back. It's a good thing we followed that cow trail home, or he'd've spotted us sure!"

Harrison! Sadie was immediately alert at the sound of his name.

"Well, what were we supposed to do, leave her out on the prairie while we fetched things? Let's get what we came for and go." The second man shuffled over to a stall, pulled up a few loose floorboards and yanked something out of its hiding spot. He stood and went to join the first man, who was bent over Sadie, looking at her like a starved dog looks at a pork chop.

How had it come to this, back in the hands of the same outlaws who'd abducted her before? And how did they know Harrison? In fact, wasn't this the very same barn he'd brought her to the night of her rescue?

She thought on this for a moment. If that was the case, then these two had to be Harrison's stepbrothers! He'd talked of them, mentioned they were (his word) "dissolute," but she hadn't met them yet. Did he have any idea they were part of the outlaw gang?

"What are we going to do with her?" Black Eye asked. Was that Jack or Sam?

"Well, we know what we're gonna do with her eventually," the other said, and they both fell into hysterics. "It's what to do with her 'tween now and then that's the question."

Black Eye leered at her with his one good eye and grabbed her ankles above her bonds. "Let's undo these here ropes and see what's under that dress." He licked his lips as his hands travelled up her legs. Sadie squirmed with revulsion at the contact.

"Not here, idjit!" the Puncher interrupted, slapping Black Eye on the back of the head. "We'll take her to the hideout and have her there. If'n we're lucky, Jeb'll be there; if he ain't, then we got her all to ourselves. Either way, he'll be happy we got rid o' her."

"Can't we just keep her? Keep her up at the hideout and use her when we want?"

The other chuckled. "Not a bad idea. But first we need to have her tell us what's in that mailbag. Can't be havin' Harrison's brothers comin' home from prison anytime soon. If that letter Harrison was so fired up to get is in there, I wanna burn it. Bad enough we're stuck with him, but somebody's gotta do the work 'round here!"

They both laughed again at that. It obviously didn't take much to set them off, and it was also obvious neither of them could read. Which meant Sadie had a chance. What sort of chance, she wasn't sure, but she'd take anything she could get right now. And that meant getting her hands on that mailbag.

Harrison jumped off Romeo and stepped onto the Wallers' porch. The front door was wide open, but the inside of the house was dark. A prickly sense of warning came over him and he instinctively drew his revolver. Something wasn't right. Where was Sadie?

"Hello?" he called into the empty hall. A tiny sound caught his attention. He cautiously entered the house and spun first to the dining room on his left, then the parlor on his right.

Sadie's mother was in the parlor, sitting in the dark, weeping.

Harrison went straight to her. "Miss Menendez! What happened? Where's Sadie?"

Teresa wiped her eyes, opened her mouth to speak, but began coughing instead.

Harrison lit a nearby oil lamp. The woman had obviously been crying for some time – her eyes were red and swollen, her face puffy. "Let me get you some water." He ran to the kitchen, where he knew a pitcher of water would be on the sideboard. He poured her a glass and hurried back to the parlor.

The woman drank greedily before speaking. "Sadie …" she rasped. "Two men …"

"What men?" Harrison asked as his body tensed.

"I don't know. I come downstairs to see what was going on. Saw the light coming through the upstairs window, could smell the smoke. Fire …"

"Yes, it woke up the whole town. But where is Sadie?"

"The door was open. I saw her outside … looking down the street." She began to cough again. Harrison patted her back until it settled. She nodded her thanks and continued. "She started to come back into the house ... and two men took her. I tried to scream, but this cough ..."

Harrison helped her take another drink before her coughing could silence her again. She couldn't cry out for help because of it, yet her hacking may have saved her life. Even if she had caught the outlaws' attention, they would likely have run rather than take a chance of being spotted. "It's all right. You witnessed what happened, and that helps. Did you see what direction they went?"

"I was coughing so hard I couldn't follow. But I think they headed south."

South? If that were the case, he should have passed them on the road when he came riding into town moments before ... unless they left the road and headed across the prairie. "Are you sure they went that way?"

"I'm sure. They didn't pass in front of the house. I don't know if they took the road or one of those cow trails. When me and the other girls first came to town, we sometimes followed them out to the prairie to pick flowers ..." Another coughing fit, another drink of water.

Harrison stood as he thought. There were two main cow trails – one led out onto the open prairie, the other back toward Harrison's farm. Could it be? He'd had his suspicions before but … "How many men did you say? Two?"

"Yes."

"Thank you, Ms. Menendez. You sit here; I'll get Grandma to take care of you."

"Harrison?" she rasped. "Find my little girl. I just got her back. I can't stand the thought of losing her again. And … and I know you feel the same."

He gave her a look of deep compassion, then smiled. "You are quite right, dear lady. And fear not, I'll find her and bring her back." Especially now that he had a good idea where to look …

He ran from the house, swung up onto Romeo, and galloped back toward the crowd of people down the street. He brought the horse to a skidding stop.

"What's the matter, Harrison? There another fire?" the sheriff shouted up at him.

"Has anyone seen my stepbrothers?"

Everyone looked around. "Nope. Ain't seen 'em," Wilfred Dunnigan offered.

"I was afraid of that," Harrison said to himself.

"What's going on?" asked Grandma.

"Miss Menendez needs you back at the house. She saw two men take Sadie and ride south."

The sheriff jumped to his feet. "Are you saying Sam and Jack took her?"

"Everyone else within a mile of town has been here, fighting the fire. I know they were in town earlier, but from the looks of it they never came home."

"They only left our place when we closed the saloon – a couple of hours ago," added Mr. Mulligan.

"Sam and Jack … don't that beat all! Sorry to hear it, Harrison," the sheriff told him. "Give me and some of the boys a minute to get our horses and let's round 'em up!"

"That's exactly what I was hoping you'd say, Sheriff. We'd better hurry – I have a pretty good idea where they might be taking her!"

The men sprang into action and quickly got their horses and guns. Grandma and Doc, meanwhile, hurried back to the house to tend Teresa and prepare for any wounded that might be brought back to town. Who knew what the night's outcome would be? In the meantime, Doc and Grandma were going to do one of the things they did best – pray.

ELEVEN

Thank the Lord for small favors! Sadie thought – in this case, the rank idiocy of her captors. Not only had they placed her and the mailbag on the same horse, but they had bound her hands in front of her, not behind her back!

Now she might have a chance. If she was very careful – and her abductors continued not to be – she could leave a trail of mail. Thus, when Harrison or anyone else came looking for her, they could follow it to the outlaws' hideout. Harrison knew where it was, but if her guess was right, no one else did. Anything would help, and the sooner she was found, the better chance she had of staying alive.

If her situation weren't so precarious, she might find it amusing: once again, her life was held in the balance by the U.S. Postal Service.

"Ain'tcha gonna blindfold her?" Jack (the one she'd previously called "Black Eye") asked. By now, she had learned which was which. They were indeed Harrison's stepbrothers, and from what she'd gathered from their conversation, their father hadn't a clue his sons were in over their heads with a band of outlaws. It seems Jack and Sam (the Puncher) kept him liquored up most of the time to avoid too many questions or inquiries as to their whereabouts, and Harrison was so inundated with farm work he didn't have time to be nosy.

She heard enough to figure out they rustled cattle for Jeb while he and some others stuck to robbing stages and wagon trains passing through to the south. It made it look like there were two separate outlaw gangs, where in reality there was only one.

"What for?" Sam answered. "She ain't comin' back."

They laughed. Sadie ignored them and eyed the mailbag hanging from the saddle horn. If she leaned forward enough while they rode, she could pull out a letter or two at a time and drop them. The darkness would shield her work, but hopefully one of her potential rescuers would still see them. *Please Lord, let it be light soon!*

"Let's go! Sooner we get up to the hideout, sooner we can have ourselves a little fun!" Sam yanked her against his chest. "I'm gonna take you first, missy," he hissed, his breath hot and rancid. She turned her face away and cringed. He laughed, kicked his horse, and they galloped out of the barn and up the road.

After a few moments, Sadie leaned forward, but Sam pulled her back again. She strained against him, trying to lean down enough to reach into the mailbag, and panic began to take hold. If she couldn't leave something for Harrison or any others to follow, it could take them much longer to find her. And time was not on her side – the outlaws were sure to kill her as soon as they were done with their "fun." She could identify both of them, and probably Jeb, their leader, as well. A witness wouldn't be tolerated.

The only thing that would buy her any time would be their use of her … but who knew how much time it would give her? And did she really want to endure that?

Perhaps death was a preferable alternative … *Oh Lord, please! Please save me*!

The arm around her tightened as her captor laughed, then licked the side of her face. She screamed into the gag and struggled, but his grip was too strong.

Out of pure desperation Sadie did the only thing she could think of. She kicked his horse. Hard.

Harrison, the sheriff and four other able-bodied men rode out of Clear Creek as if their lives depended on it. In this case, it was Sadie's life at stake, and Harrison was determined to save it.

He'd often wondered over the last year if his stepbrothers had anything to do with the current crime wave in the area, not to mention the unsavory events that led to his two older brothers, Duncan and Colin, being arrested over a year and a half ago. Until now, he hadn't any proof of their guilt – Jack and Sam always had some sort of alibi when livestock went missing.

Still, it was obvious that Duncan and Colin had been lured into the wrong place at the wrong time and framed for cattle rustling off a wagon train. Harrison had managed to get new information from his stepfather that had set him on the trail of the real bandits. But none of that mattered at the moment – right now, rescuing Sadie was his only goal.

They reined in their horses a mile out of town at his signal. "We should split up. They may have gone back to the farm or, if my guess is right, they've gone to the cabin above the ridge. But we can't be sure which."

"Henry, you pick two of the boys and check Harrison's farm," ordered the sheriff. "The rest of us will follow Harrison up to the ridge."

"If they're at the farm, be ever so careful. Ride after us and fire off a few shots to signal you've found her. We'll come join you."

"Will do, Harrison! Butch, Andy – follow me!" Henry said as he and two others spun his horse around and took off toward Harrison's farm.

"If she's there, Henry'll know what to do," the sheriff reassured.

Harrison nodded, turned his horse, and the remaining three headed across the prairie. After about ten minutes, he signaled for a stop. They listened carefully for gunshots and, when none were forthcoming, once again sped toward the line of pines in the distance.

Harrison had guessed right – they hadn't taken her to the farm, but to their cabin hideout. Hopefully. He prayed in earnest as they rode in the pre-dawn darkness: that the outlaws had only the one hideout, and that they would reach Sadie before any of the dirty scoundrels had a chance to touch her. If any of them, even ... no, *especially* his stepbrothers, touched a single hair on her head, he'd see them hanged higher than Haman. And maybe shot for good measure. But he couldn't let such murderous thoughts cloud his thinking, he knew – he needed his wits about him.

By the time they reached the tree line, though, he'd imagined several more clever ways to exact justice on his stepbrothers.

"Which way?" huffed the sheriff as they brought their horses to a stop. The sky was just starting to lighten in the east.

The animals were breathing hard and steaming by now. Harrison knew that they would need their strength to make it up to the ridge. "Best to walk the horses for a bit. It's about two, maybe two and a half miles up through the trees. There's a stream nearby – we can leave the horses there."

The sheriff nodded and they set off, Harrison in the lead. He let Romeo pick his way along a deer trail that led through the pines and alders. But soon it faded, and the horses had to find their own way through the ever-thickening trees and brush. Occasionally, they would stop and listen for sounds of other horses crashing through the wood, but there were none. His brothers must have had enough of a head start to have already reached the cabin. Sweat popped out on Harrison's brow with the thought. He risked the noise he knew it would make, and pushed Romeo a little harder.

Soon he heard the sound of water. They headed for it and, when they reached the stream, found a suitable spot to leave the horses. The men dismounted and checked their guns. Harrison studied the trees around them. "There was a stand of alder several hundred yards from the cabin. It shouldn't be far from here. If we head upstream, we'll come to it."

The men nodded and followed. Sure enough, a minute later they reached the stand of trees Harrison remembered and began to cautiously make their way along another deer trail that led away from the stream.

Before long, they reached their destination. Harrison dropped to his belly behind a fallen log and signaled the others to do the same. They could see the cabin through the trees, smoke rising from the chimney in lazy blue tendrils. "We've got to get them away from her somehow," he whispered.

The sheriff peeked over the tree. "I don't suppose one of your animal calls is gonna work this time?"

Harrison grimaced. "Jack and Sam may not be the smartest, but they do have memories. They'll not fall for that twice." He surveyed the area around the cabin. Only two horses were in the rickety corral, and all was quiet. A good sign. He knew that if he heard Sadie begin to scream, he would likely go mad. "We could set the cabin on fire," he mused.

"Not a bad idea. It'd get them out of there quick-like."

"There's a back door. I'll make my way around to it; you and Bart go to the front and set the cabin aflame. While they're distracted, I'll run in and get Miss Jones."

"They won't hurt her, will they? Use her as a shield?"

"If I know Jack and Sam, they'll rush to save their own skins. Neither of them will think quickly enough to use Miss Jones to barter with."

The sheriff and Bart nodded, and went to work making torches out of whatever they could find. Within moments, they had what they needed and each man began to get into position.

Harrison, meanwhile, was crawling on his belly as he circled around through the trees to the back of the cabin. It had been much easier the previous time, when it was dark. Now that the sun was rising, he had to be extra careful not to be seen.

As soon as he was out of sight, the sheriff and Bart slunk their way to the structure, lit their torches of dried pine branches and threw them on top of the roof. In moments, the fire had engulfed the shingles.

Harrison, gun drawn, tiptoed to the back door and listened. Nothing. Not a sound except the fire crackling and roaring overhead. Then he heard a roof beam snap and cringed. Good Lord, what if they were asleep or passed out drunk? And Sadie was undoubtedly bound and gagged …

Knowing he had to act fast, he burst through the back door. By now the cabin was full of smoke, and the flames on the roof were making their way inside. "Sadie! Sadie?" he called through the haze. He coughed, and pulled his bandana over his nose and mouth as he frantically searched the main room, then ran into the room where he'd first seen Sadie bound to a chair. No one. He checked the smaller third room. Still nothing.

"Oh, Lord, no," he whispered as realization dawned. He ran back into the main room and opened the front door. The sheriff and Bart stood outside, their guns aimed at him. "Don't shoot! It's me, Harrison!"

They lowered their guns. "Where in tarnation are they?" the sheriff called over the roar of the fire, confused.

"Not here!" Harrison managed between coughs as he ran from the porch.

"But what about them horses?" Bart asked.

Harrison looked at the two horses panicking in the corral, and silently cursed himself for his stupidity. "Those aren't Jack and Sam's."

"Well, if no one's here, and those horses aren't Jack and Sam's, then where are they?" the sheriff lamented.

Harrison brushed past the sheriff as he began to scan the area. "I wish I knew …"

Sadie fought back tears as Jack roughly carried her through the trees. They'd gone to the cabin as she'd expected, but only stayed long enough to get a few things.

The cabin had been stripped bare. Apparently, some of the other outlaws were still nearby, their horses in the small corral, a fire slowly dying inside the fireplace from before dawn. A note had been left telling those who were able to meet up at the "other" hideout where they would make plans for their next job. Sam had ungagged her only long enough for her to read the message to them. Then Jack and Sam had gathered some blankets that were left and a cast iron kettle, and headed off into the woods further up the ridge.

They rode for at least half an hour before they came to another makeshift corral, but there was no cabin to be seen. The men had tied up their horses and continued on foot, Sadie slung over Jack's shoulder. She occasionally grunted when Jack stumbled on a rock or root, but otherwise tried to stay silent during the rough trek to wherever it was they were going, while wondering how far it could be.

She didn't want to do anything more to provoke the men. Sam had been so mad when she'd kicked his horse – almost getting both of them thrown off – that he'd stopped, dismounted, yanked her off and put a knife to her throat. She would have been killed right there if Jack hadn't talked his brother down out of his rage. Finally Jack, probably deeming her defilement more important than his brother's temper, had thrown her over the saddle, well out of reach of the mailbag. That left no way to leave a trail. It didn't help that Jack would occasionally smack her rump and regaled her with all the dire things he'd planned for her unwilling carcass.

Finally they arrived. Jack's heavy breathing slowed as he dropped her onto the hard ground. He bent over her and tried to catch his breath as Sam, mail bag on one shoulder, blankets rolled up and slung with a rope over the other, set the kettle down next to her.

Sadie looked at it, then glared at Sam. Maybe if she acted bravely, she'd feel the same way.

Sam leered at her. "Yer mine, missy. And I'm gonna enjoy every inch o' you." He wiped his mouth with the back of his hand.

"Hey, what about me? I carried her all the way up here. I should get her first!" Jack argued.

"You're too tired. Besides, ya don't want her first. I'll get her all warmed up for ya. She'll be sweeter when she's broke in a little."

Jack pulled her to her feet. "I said, I want her first!"

Sam shoved him and she fell to the ground. They had retied her ankles, apparently not wanting to chance her escaping on foot. Perhaps they weren't the best runners. She kept that bit of information in mind as Sam yanked her back up and hefted her onto his shoulder. "Let's go."

Jack grumbled, picked up the rest of their effects and followed along like an obedient dog. After a few moments, they went around a small stand of trees and came upon what looked like the entrance to a mine shaft. Sadie caught a glimpse of it as Sam turned to look around before they entered the darkness.

Inside, the air suddenly became still and cold. She didn't like the way the darkness swallowed them up so quickly, and began to struggle.

"Stop that! Mind yerself!" Sam scolded as he slapped her hard on the rump. His large hand stung, and she stilled her movements. Unable to help herself, the tears finally broke free. At least in the pitch blackness, they wouldn't be able to see her fear. Maybe she'd get lucky and there would be no light when they performed their heinous deeds on her body and then murdered her. Perhaps it would all be easier to stomach in the dark …

No. She knew better. It would be horrible regardless.

Lord, help me!

TWELVE

Sadie fell to the ground in a heap. She listened as the two men rustled about in the darkness before she heard the distinct sound of a match being lit. She had to squint against the light as Sam took a lantern from a large rock and lit it. He adjusted it and hung it from a nail protruding from a beam as she squinted at their surroundings.

They were indeed inside some sort of mine shaft – a dead end, from the looks of it. The space was maybe twelve feet square, reinforced with some posts and beams. She didn't notice any fresh marks in the rock that would indicate it was in active use. Several barrels sat against one wall, with a couple bales of hay, a sack of grain and some crates and boxes against the others.

Sam went to one of the barrels, took off the lid and brought out a whiskey bottle. He pulled the cork out with his teeth, took a long swallow, wiped his mouth with the back of his hand and leered.

The dark chill returned to Sadie's spine.

"Go take a look around," Sam ordered Jack. "See if anyone else has come up yet."

Jack dumped his load to the ground. The kettle hit a rock and the noise echoed off the walls. "Why do I gotta take a look around? We was just outside!"

Sam spun on him. "Git out! Go outside while I ..." He turned back to Sadie, eyes glazed with lust. "... while I get her ready for ya."

"Ain't no reason I can't have her first!" Jack growled. "You take everythin' first!"

Sam punched him square in the gut, doubling Jack over in pain. "I said, git! Take a look and make sure no one followed us!"

Jack straightened, eyes full of rage. "Better hurry it up, 'cause I aim to take my time with her!" He turned and stomped back to the mine's entrance. Sadie watched as he disappeared into the darkness. It looked like *her* time was running out.

Sam grabbed her by the wrists and dragged her to the center of the cave, then reached for the blankets they'd brought and began to untie them. He looked around, deciding where to spread them, then threw them down behind the barrels. Apparently even a hardened criminal liked his privacy while committing the unthinkable. Returning to her, he pulled her to her feet. "Now, missy," he drawled, his breath reeking of whisky, "let's you and me have ourselves a time."

He picked her up, carried her behind the barrels and threw her down, then straddled her hips to hold her in place. He pierced her with such an inhuman look of lust that it made her go cold. Her whole body went numb with fear as he tried to kiss her through the gag, then twisted around to cut the bonds on her ankles. Grinning as he turned back, he grabbed her bound wrists and held them above her head, then undid his gun belt with his other hand, pulled it off and threw it aside. The belt holding up his pants soon followed it.

He grunted in frustration as he fumbled with her clothing in an attempt to rip the bodice of her dress open. He cursed when it didn't yield, then pulled a knife and held it to her throat. "This is all gonna have to come off, missy." He smiled as he poked the point through the collar of her dress with the knife and began to slice it away.

Sadie braced herself. If she was going to die anyway, she'd rather fight him and have him slit her throat than meekly endure what Sam was planning ...

Click.

Sadie and Sam both froze at the sound. *Could it be ...?*

"Take your filthy hands off her, Sam. Or I shall have no recourse but to paint the walls with your brains."

Harrison stood behind Sam, a gun to the back of his stepbrother's head. His face was locked in determined rage. Sadie smiled in relief, not feeling one bit sorry for the outlaw.

Sam dropped the knife and put his hands in the air. Harrison snatched it up, threw it into the darkness, then yanked Sam off Sadie and pinned him against the wall, the gun in his face. "Give me one good reason – why shouldn't I shoot you right now?"

Sadie lay frozen in place. She'd never seen a man so fiercely angry.

"What's the matter, Harrison?" Sam had the nerve to drawl. "Afraid I'd ruin her 'fore you got the chance?"

Sadie instinctively closed her eyes.

Harrison slammed the butt of his revolver into Sam's face. "Any other witty *bon mots*, brother?" He let go, and watched Sam slump bonelessly to the ground. "I thought not. Cur." He holstered his gun, bent down and shoved Sam up against the rock wall, as far away from Sadie as he could get him.

Then and only then did he turn to her. "Are you all right, princess?"

I will be, she thought weakly, willing herself not to faint.

Gently, Harrison picked her up, carried her to the middle of the cave and set her on her feet. He wrapped her in his arms and held her tight, mumbling something unintelligible into her hair.

Sadie tried to say "thank you" – and only then did both of them realize she was still gagged. "Oh. Terribly sorry," Harrison said in embarrassment, and quickly removed the bandana and handkerchief from her mouth. Sadie gulped air, perhaps a little too quickly as her knees went weak.

Harrison, thankfully, caught her before she could drop.

And now she began to weep in earnest, from the trauma of the night and morning, the realization that she'd be dead if not for Harrison, and the relief that hopefully it was now over.

He held her to him, stroking her hair. "There now, princess," he whispered. "You're safe now. They can't hurt you anymore. I'm here." He kissed her forehead, her ear, her cheek. His lips were soft and warm against her skin. She couldn't think or speak, and didn't want to. Having him hold her, as her body began to shake uncontrollably, was enough.

It was a couple of minutes before Sadie could stop spasming and sobbing. But when she did, she suddenly realized that her hands, still bound in front of her, were accidentally pressed against a particular – and highly inappropriate! – portion of Harrison Cooke's anatomy. "Oh dear!" she exclaimed, pulling away suddenly. "I didn't mean ... I just ... sorry, I ..."

"Sh," Harrison said sharply. He unsheathed his own knife, cut the rope around her wrists, and began rubbing her hands to bring back the circulation. "It's quite all right, under the circumstances."

"W-what do you mean?" she asked, confused.

He looked into her eyes, and she could see the love alight in his face. "Sadie Jones, I know this is hardly the romantic setting one would hope for. But I love you madly, and I want you to be my wife, forever and anon. And if you say yes, rest assured that not only will I never let any harm come to you, ever again, but that I will never object to any place you choose to put your hands."

Sadie had been through too much over the past several days to hesitate at such an offer. "Yes, yes!" she cried, throwing her arms around his neck.

He kissed her then, not the soft and tentative kiss of the fearful suitor, but a kiss of resolution, of promises, of protection. Of possession. She was his and his alone, and he was just as equally hers. No arguments, no complaints, no hesitation. It was a kiss that spoke of lifetimes, and of eternity.

And Sadie reveled in the knowledge that with a single kiss he had claimed her so completely, and banished her fear so thoroughly. She could live on a kiss like this. A moment before, she had been resigning herself to death; now she was ready to stand against the armies of the world, so long as it was under this man's banner.

Harrison finally broke the kiss and held her tightly to him. "I love you, Sadie Jones. I've loved you from the first moment I saw you." He looked into her eyes and captured her again. "I've nothing to offer – no lands, no title, no money, a dozen or so pigs that I don't even own. But you'll have my heart as long as I live, and beyond into the hereafter. I'll love you with all my strength and being."

Before Sadie could answer, a low moan echoed from a corner of the cave.

Nope, not this time, she thought. Without batting an eye she let go of Harrison, stomped over to where Sam was beginning to rouse, and kicked him in the back of the head. Sam went limp and silent again. Satisfied with the result, she returned, locked her arms around Harrison's neck and pulled him down for another kiss.

How long it lasted, neither one knew. But neither was inclined to stop … at least

until the sheriff came upon them. "Um …
sorry to interrupt …"

Harrison reluctantly lifted his face from
hers. "I love you, my princess," he
whispered and kissed her forehead again.
"My brave and beautiful prairie princess.
And now I'm going to make you my
queen." He held out his arm, she took it,
and they followed the sheriff outside.

Sadie sat up in bed and let Doc examine
her. The ride back to town had been slow.
They had come out of the cave to find Jack
on his knees, hands over his head and
several guns pointed at him. Both Jack and
Sam were handcuffed, tethered by a length
of rope to the saddle horns of their horses
– which were led by Andy and Bart from
the posse, and forced to walk all the way
back to town. It was especially rough on
Sam, who had a splitting headache.

Sadie rode with Harrison astride
Romeo, her dress wrapped about her legs,
her body leaning against Harrison's broad
chest. She slept part of the way once they
reached the prairie, and awoke with a start

as she realized something. "How did you find me?" They were the first words she'd spoken since leaving the mine shaft.

He sat up straighter and wrapped his other arm around her. "I followed your trail, dear heart."

"My trail? What trail?"

Harrison chuckled. "The mail, of course! Once we found it, it led us right to you. Very clever, princess."

"Wait ... the *mail*? I wanted to use the mail, but I never got the chance!"

"Well ... there was a trail of it all the same. In fact, if it hadn't been there, we may not have found you for hours."

Then she remembered. When Sam threatened to kill her, his knife caught on something as he pulled it from his boot. It must have been the mailbag – he'd accidentally torn it. The mail must've been falling out through the tear one letter at a time, and none of them had even realized it.

Now Sadie started laughing, with joy. The good Lord *had* been watching over her! And she didn't stop laughing for the remainder of the journey back to town.

"Nothing broken, just a few bumps and bruises," Doc announced.

Harrison stood at the end of the bed. "Thank the Lord for that!"

"You go on down to the kitchen and let her rest. Grandma's got something on the stove." Doc waved Harrison toward the door.

Suddenly there was a commotion downstairs. "Here now!" they heard Grandma exclaim. "You can't just barge in here! Who do you think you are?"

Someone came stomping up the stairs. Sadie's eyes immediately grew wide. She knew only one person who would storm into a house like that …

Horatio Jones burst into the bedroom in a huff. "Sadie! There you are! What's going on? Why are you in bed? Get your things together, pronto!"

Doc stood in open-mouthed shock. Harrison, on the other hand, crossed his arms, his eyes narrowed to slits.

Sadie looked at all three men, and swallowed hard. "Hello, Papa."

"Don't you 'hello, Papa' me, young lady! You've got a lot of explaining to do!"

"And I'm sure she shall be quite willing to explain everything, Mr. Jones,"

Harrison replied, his shoulders squared and his jaw set. "After she's rested."

Her father noted the stance, and bristled. "And who are you?"

"Harrison Cooke, at your service. Miss Jones's betrothed."

"Her … *what?*" Horatio asked, his jaw dropping.

"Her betrothed," Harrison repeated and glanced quickly in her direction. She nodded at her father. "Sadie has been through something of an ordeal, and is under physician's order to rest until fully recovered. She would appreciate your cooperation in this, and I would be happy to continue this discussion downstairs in the parlor."

Harrison's flowery verbiage seemed to slow Horatio Jones down a bit. He looked Harrison up and down in confusion. "Where in blazes are you from? No one around here talks like that! Oh, gad! Don't tell me you're one of those fancy fellas! No daughter of mine is gonna tie the knot with some dandy!"

He looked to Sadie, his eyes suddenly wide with horror. "You don't *have* to be marrying him do you?"

Sadie smiled. "Perhaps not, Papa! But I plan to, nonetheless."

Horatio Jones looked Harrison over a second time, suddenly seeming a bit outgunned. "Who ... where did ... consarn it, what in Sam Hill is going on here?! Who *are* you?!"

"Harrison Nathaniel Cooke, at your service," he told him and bowed.

"Oh, gads! You *are* a dandy! You may not be wearing fancy clothes, but you're a dandy just the same!" He quickly turned on Sadie. "The only fancy dude around for hundreds of miles and you find him! I bet he can't even shoot!"

"Oh, he can shoot all right!" said Doc. "Harrison and his two brothers are some of the best shots in this part of the territory!"

"Gads! There's *more* of them?"

"Papa, please, he's not what you think," said Sadie. Her father looked at her, completely aghast.

"I understand this may all be rather unnerving," Harrison said calmly, motioning Horatio to a chair next to Sadie's bed. "But I believe that after you have been acquainted with the events of the last several days, it will all be clear."

Horatio dropped into the chair like a steer being hit in the head with a sledgehammer. "If you say so, son." He shook his head and turned to Sadie. "Him?" he asked, jerking his thumb over his shoulder at Harrison.

Sadie laughed, despite her exhaustion. "Papa. I love him, and I'm going to marry him. If it hadn't been for Harrison, I'd be dead now."

That got his attention. His face drained of color. "That dandy saved your life?" he said, incredulous.

"Twice," Sadie affirmed. "And I doubt the outlaws he tracked several miles into the wilderness thought he was a dandy."

"Really?" Now Horatio looked up at Harrison with a new respect. "But still, Sadie, that don't mean you have to get hitched ..."

"She loves him, *Horacio*," a voice spoke from the doorway. "That should be reason enough."

All heads turned toward Sadie's mother. She entered the room slowly, never taking her eyes off of Horatio.

It took a second, but a spark of recognition lit in Horatio's eyes. "Oh my ..."

"Papa," Sadie began. "This is …"

"I know who this is," Horatio interrupted. "Teresa …"

"And here I thought you'd forgotten about me," Teresa said, one eyebrow raised.

Horatio's eyes took on a faraway look. "I'd never forget you," he whispered, then rubbed his hand over his face. "I don't know about anyone else, but I think I need a drink."

"I'm afraid you're a victim of bad timing, sir," Harrison calmly informed him. "Before we could catch the outlaws, they burned the saloon down. Accidentally, so I'm told, but burned down nonetheless."

"Figures," Horatio groaned, then looked over at Sadie again. "What kind of a crazy town is this?"

"A town where I could spend the rest of my life with the man I love," Sadie spoke softly.

Teresa smiled, tears in her eyes. Harrison reached her in a few quick strides and put his arm around her. "I was going to ask you for your blessing, Ms. Menendez."

Teresa nodded, unable to speak.

"But with both her parents here, so much the better!" he concluded.

Horatio seemed to be trying desperately not to slip into shock. "I, I don't feel right about this at all. Sadie, go get your things – we're leaving!"

Teresa suddenly straightened. "She's not going anywhere, *Horacio*! She's been abducted, nearly killed, and threatened with the worst things a woman can be threatened with! You leave her be!"

Horatio turned white. He closed his eyes and swallowed hard. "Sadie ... I was so afraid I'd lost you. When we couldn't find you ..." He shuddered. "I was about to go out of my mind, girl!"

Sadie leaned toward him and placed her hand on his. "I'm sorry if I scared you, Papa. But I'm fine now – Harrison saw to that. I love him with all my heart. And," she added, pointing to Teresa, "I found Mama. She was dying, but the Lord made her well again."

Horatio took in the sight of Teresa standing next to Harrison, and his face softened. "I suppose I owe you an apology, young man. You saved my daughter's life. And Teresa ... I *know* I owe you an apology. Can you forgive me?"

Teresa frowned in thought. "I may need a little time ... but yes."

"And I accept your apology as well," Harrison said heartily. "Now, Mr. Jones, perhaps we should repair to the parlor – we have much to talk about. And I'm sure Dr. Waller has some ... medicinal spirits around here somewhere ..."

EPILOGUE

Four months later ...

"Yeeeee-haw! Here they come!" Henry Fig yelled as he galloped through town. A thunderous roar could be heard behind him. Everyone ran out into the street to watch.

"No, no! Get off the street! You people want to get killed?" the sheriff yelled. The townsfolk quickly got out of the way as they felt the ground shake.

Within moments, hundreds of cattle came into view, driven by the men of the Big J – over a thousand head of some of the finest beasts anyone in Clear Creek had ever seen. But to Horatio Jones, it was simply a little wedding present to Mr. and Mrs. Harrison Cooke, whose ranch (formerly a pig farm) was located south of town.

Sadie and Harrison watched their new stock – or at least part of it, a few hundred – lumber through town. The rest had been driven by another route back to their new ranch, while these headed to a corral Harrison had built at the other end of Clear Creek. He'd wanted to give some to the sheriff and his men for helping him rescue Sadie and bring his stepbrothers to justice. He also planned on selling each person in town a steer, at well below market price, to help them out for the following winter. It was the gentlemanly thing to do.

"Do you think you'll like cattle ranching?" Sadie yelled over the sound of hundreds of hooves trotting along the street below them. They were on the balcony of the second floor of Mulligan's new saloon.

"I'll enjoy it, I'm sure! Your father is a very generous man!" Harrison replied in dramatic understatement. Horatio Jones, for all his bluster and bewilderment, had finally consented to letting Sadie marry Harrison, but had insisted on helping the young couple start out properly. Harrison thought that meant a bit of livestock and perhaps helping him spruce up his family's farm. But Horatio never thought that small. Instead, he'd built them a new ranch house, a new barn, a little cabin for Harrison's stepfather ... and now eleven hundred head of cattle, give or take a few. It was unheard of, but here they were.

"Always did prefer a good steak to ham," Colin Cooke said as he joined them.

"I still like ham," Duncan, the eldest Cooke, added. "But I shan't be picky."

Harrison put his arms around his two older brothers. "Looks like we're in the cattle trade now, chaps."

"Anything's better than rotting in gaol, Harrison – give me a branding iron over leg irons any day!" Colin sighed. "You're the best brother, Harry. Mother would be proud."

"You can thank Sadie's father for speaking with the warden himself. Not to mention writing the governor."

"We can't thank him enough for all he's done on our behalf – and yours," Duncan said. "And certainly Clear Creek will never be the same because of him. I have a feeling this little town is going to start growing now."

"It already has," Colin added, waving an arm at the torrent of cattle below them. He turned to his new sister-in-law. "Will your mother be visiting again soon?"

Sadie smiled. "She and my father will be getting married next month. I asked them to have the wedding here, in the new church."

"But … we don't have a clergyman yet," Duncan said.

"There's one coming from the Nebraska Territory. He's the son of one of my father's friends, and also knows Mr. Van Cleet. He'll be here in time for the wedding."

"Colin was right. Our little town is indeed already growing," said Harrison with a smile.

They continued to watch until the last steer thundered past on the street below. Harrison removed his arms from around his brothers' shoulders, put them around his wife and kissed her. "Well, princess, let's go have a look at our wedding present."

They left. Duncan and Colin continued to watch as the dust settled and the townsfolk followed the cattle to the corral.

"I suppose we should go help out," Duncan suggested.

"I suppose so," Colin replied.

Duncan turned and headed downstairs. Colin was about to follow when the stage came rolling in, pulling up in front of Dunnigan's Mercantile. Colin watched as Wilfred and Irene came rushing out. Irene Dunnigan looked exceedingly happy, which raised Colin's suspicions. He decided to stay put and see what all the excitement was about – from a safe distance.

A young woman got out of the stage.

Even from such a remove, he could see she was incredibly beautiful – a Greek marble come to life. His mouth suddenly went dry and his breathing stopped. If there was ever such a thing as love at first sight, then this was it.

But then he saw the heavenly creature hugging Irene and kissing her on the cheek. "Oh dear," he mumbled. This beauty must be a relative of the Dunnigans. Which meant that Irene Dunnigan would be in charge of her.

Colin's heart almost sank. Almost. Because if there was one thing he enjoyed, it was a challenge – he liked to brag that as an Englishman, he was descended from a long line of empire-builders and dragon-slayers. And no one in Clear Creek could dispute the fact that Irene Dunnigan was more than the usual challenge.

To win that young lady's heart, Colin Cooke mused with a smile, he would have to live up to the reputation of his dragon-slaying forebears …

The End

I hope you enjoyed *His Prairie Princess*.
Other books in the series include:

Her Prairie Knight (Prairie Brides, Book Two)
His Prairie Duchess (Prairie Brides, Book
Three)
Her Prairie Viking (Prairie Brides, Book
Four)
His Prairie Sweetheart (Prairie Brides, Book
Five)
Her Prairie Outlaw (Prairie Brides, Book Six)
Christmas in Clear Creek (Prairie Brides,
Book Seven)

Thank you for reading ~

ABOUT THE AUTHOR

Kit Morgan, aka Geralyn Beauchamp, loves a good Western. Her father loved them as well, and they watched their fair share together over the years. You can keep up-to-date on future books, fun contests and more at Kit Morgan's website:
www.authorkitmorgan.com.

Be sure to sign up for her newsletter to keep up to date on future books and fun contests!